THE ULTIMATE UNOFFICIAL ENCYCLOPEDIA FOR MINECRAFTERS

MULTIPLAYER MODE

THE ULTIMATE UNOFFICIAL ENCYCLOPEDIA FOR MINECRAFTERS

MULTIPLAYER MODE

EXPLORING HIDDEN GAMES AND SECRET WORLDS

CARA J. STEVENS

Sky Pony Press
New York

Sky Pony Press books may be purchased in bulk at special discounts for sales promotion, corporate gifts, fund-raising, or educational purposes. Special editions can also be created to specifications. For details, contact the Special Sales Department, Sky Pony Press, 307 West 36th Street, 11th Floor, New York, NY 10018 or info@skyhorsepublishing.com.

Minecraft® is a registered trademark of Notch Development AB.
The Minecraft game is copyright © Mojang AB.

Visit our website at www.skyponypress.com.
Authors, books, and more at SkyPonyPressBlog.com.

10 9 8 7 6 5 4 3 2 1

Library of Congress Cataloging-in-Publication Data is available on file.

Cover design by Brian Peterson
Cover art by Cara J. Stevens, Nicky Vermeersch, and Ben Pineau

Excerpts from "11 Family-Friendly Minecraft Servers Where Your Kid Can Play Safely Online" (June 3, 2014), reprinted with permission from Matt Doyle of Brightpips.com. For the complete article, go to www.brightpips.com/11-family-friendly-minecraft-servers-where-your-kid-can-play-safely-online.

"A Note About Safety," pages two through four, provided by Michelle Hernandez and Caroline Knorr of Common Sense Media.org.

Print ISBN: 978-1-5107-1816-6
Ebook ISBN: 978-1-5107-1825-8

Printed in China

SPECIAL THANKS TO THE FOLLOWING CONTRIBUTORS:

Mattias Neid at Aternos, https://aternos.org/en

Adam Selke at Evolve HQ online gaming, www.evolvehq.com

Michelle Hernandez and Caroline Knorr of Common Sense Media

My team of young Minecrafters: Charmander MC, Jack P, TennisBrandon, Nate33339, mrcool9

Matt Doyle, Brightpips

Nicky (q220) Vermeersch, Minecraft Middle Earth

Jimmy (Kryptix_), Omnikraft

David Wasman, MCMagic Parks

Fred Borcherdt

Ben Pineau

TECHNICAL REQUIREMENTS: LET'S GET STARTED!

The information provided in this book refers to features in the PC edition of Minecraft 1.10.2. While there are some family-friendly servers for the Pocket Edition and Xbox versions of Minecraft, the vast majority of servers work with the PC/Mac version. If you are using a different version, you may find some differences in gameplay and may not be able to join at all. To join a multiplayer game, you will need to have a valid, paid-for version of the game. If your game is **cracked**, pirated, or stolen, you will not be able to join servers or access most multiplayer features. When joining a **server**, you do not need to download any special **mods** (**modifications**) or **plugins** ahead of time. Servers already have the plugins uploaded so you simply need to sign up, log in, and play. If you have mods installed, beware. Most servers ban at least some mods—particularly those that let you cheat. Usually, mods that help your game run more smoothly are allowed.

INTRODUCTION

WELCOME TO THE MULTIPLAYER MINECRAFT EXPERIENCE

If you're reading this, chances are you've already mastered your own universe through building, fighting, farming, inventing, and living in the Minecraft world and you're ready to venture out into playing online with others. Within the pages of this encyclopedia, you'll learn how to get online to expand your Minecraft universe and get even more out of your gameplay. We'll show you how to create a private network or join one already in progress, and once you're online, you'll find places to build collaboratively, join an online village or community, play hosted mini-games, create unique gaming experiences, work together to overcome the perils and pitfalls of Minecraft Survival mode, have gaming parties, and explore all the other possibilities of an open platform.

As you go through the entries in this book, you'll get step-by-step instructions on how to safely join worlds already in play, find new servers to explore, and learn about different types of games and online experiences to make gaming an even more exciting adventure.

Which Multiplayer Mode Is Right for You?
Each one of these three Multiplayer modes brings its own brand of fun. Keep it simple on a home network or venture out into public communities where you can play alongside gamers from across the globe.

Choose from the following:

1. Play with friends in your own home network
2. Play on a private realm or server
3. Join an online multiplayer community

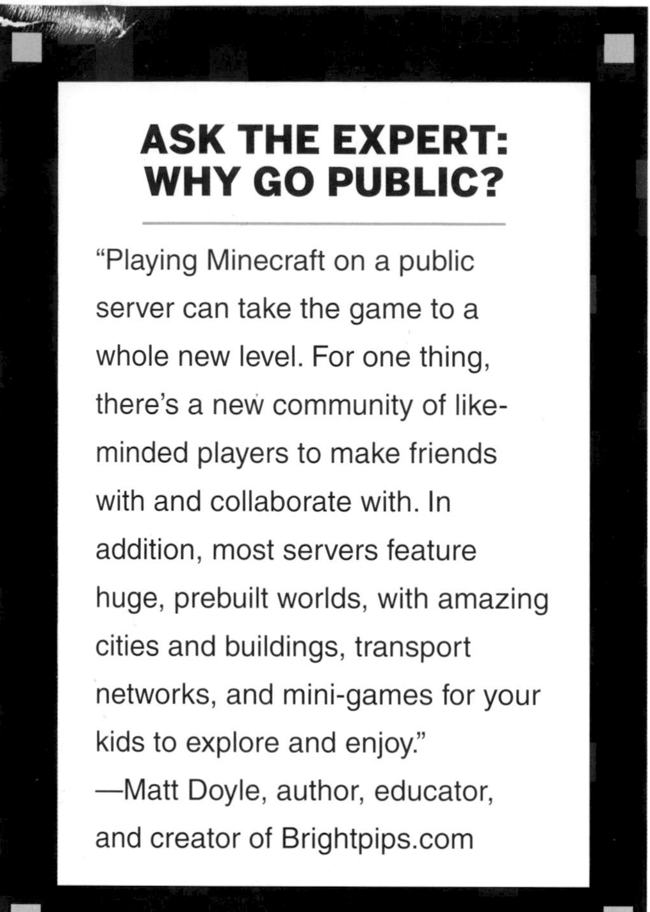

ASK THE EXPERT: WHY GO PUBLIC?

"Playing Minecraft on a public server can take the game to a whole new level. For one thing, there's a new community of like-minded players to make friends with and collaborate with. In addition, most servers feature huge, prebuilt worlds, with amazing cities and buildings, transport networks, and mini-games for your kids to explore and enjoy."
—Matt Doyle, author, educator, and creator of Brightpips.com

A NOTE ABOUT SAFETY

Once you jump into a multiplayer environment, you may feel like you're being transported into another world—a faraway world that has nothing to do with the real world. But when you meet, team up, chat, and play with players online, you need to always keep in mind that the people with whom you're playing are real, live people just like you. Multiplayer gameplay, or MMOs, can offer great opportunities for teamwork, group problem-solving, and building or strengthening friendships. But, as with any online activity, you should be aware of the risks and cautious of how you act.

Interacting with strangers can be loads of fun, but it can also be a little risky. Here are some key points to keep in mind when you play online.

Interactions with Strangers

When you belong to an online community—such as those related to Minecraft, LEGO, and the Hunger Games—you don't always know the real identities of the other members. Follow these rules to stay safe:

- It's okay to meet up online with pals from the "real world." If you meet someone and discover you're both, say, Pokémon fans, ask for each other's usernames and make plans to meet up online on a specific server at a set time.
- ALWAYS have your parents check every game (or site or app) for features that let you customize the game for your ability, age, family rules, and so on. Games often offer

many options to boost safety, and if you're under seventeen, your settings should always be confirmed by an adult.

- ALWAYS keep your parents in the loop when you interact with people online and let your folks know immediately if you are contacted by a stranger or if you've had to delete or block a friend, acquaintance, or fellow player you met online.
- NEVER agree or initiate plans to meet a stranger offline or outside of gameplay (over the phone, email, Skype, or anywhere other than the whitelisted server where you play).
- NEVER share personally identifiable information, like your real name, address, phone number, or any other personal information, with a stranger online.
- NEVER share your passwords, even with friends. Keeping your password protected is essential to online safety. When you hand over your password, you're giving someone the ability to pose as you online, use (or misuse) your stuff, and mess with your achievements.

HARASSMENT FROM OTHER PLAYERS

Online communities such as Minecraft are bonded by a common purpose and servers are moderated, which keeps bad behavior in check. And, even though many virtual worlds have rules about behavior, some kids and adults find ways around these rules. Talk with your parents and read the site rules before you play so that you'll know when an interaction is just friendly PvP (Player versus Player) play and when it's harassment, "griefing," or another form of cyberbullying.

- Make sure your parents set privacy settings that are age-appropriate to keep you safe. Privacy settings for kids' games should give you the ability to block people, flag misbehavior, and limit the kinds of communication kids can have (some games allow "free chat" and some let you choose chat phrases from a list). The servers listed in this book have strict rules and some have permissions to set as well as moderators who keep an eye on everything, but not all servers you come across in search engines or online provide the same level of protection.

- Always be on your best behavior. A good rule of thumb: If you wouldn't say something to someone's face, you shouldn't say it online.
- Let an adult know about any unwanted contact with people online, such as swearing, threats, or excessive attacks on your character in the game. Don't play against kids who are mean to you.
- Read the server rules to find out how to flag inappropriate conduct. Ask an adult to show you how to use the flagging feature if you can't figure it out. Even if you feel you can handle what's happening in the game, flagging inappropriate behavior is a great example of being a good citizen and showing you care about others. This is a healthy way to keep social-networking sites safe and fun for everyone.

BALANCING GAME TIME WITH OTHER ACTIVITIES

A big challenge for anyone who enters an online gaming world is finding a balance between playing in online worlds—which can draw you in for long periods—and enjoying plenty of offline family and social time. Even "good" games can become a problem when homework, chores, family obligations, and real-world social activities end up taking a backseat and you can't—or won't—stop playing. Even if you feel like you're learning from the game, racking up achievements, helping others, or making great progress, make sure you don't neglect the other areas of your life that demand your attention.

—Caroline Knorr, senior parenting editor, Common Sense Media

HOW TO JOIN A MINECRAFT SERVER

There are three ways to get online for a multiplayer gaming experience. Once you know what they are and how to set up each network, you'll be free to enjoy Minecraft with other kids who love it as much as you do.

1. LAN

A LAN is a local area network, also known as your home network or wifi connection. Gameplay over LAN is completely private. If you have friends or family at your house, you can each play on a different computer as long as you're all connected to the same network.

2. Public or Private Server

You can open Minecraft on your home computer and use it as a private server for friends to join even if they're not on your home network, or you can connect to an online public server. When you connect to a public server, you can play with strangers from all over the world. On a busy server, you'll almost always find people to play with, but you have to be more careful and follow rules more strictly.

3. Minecraft Realms

Mojang, the creators of Minecraft, offers a subscription service called Minecraft Realms that lets you invite people to come join your world. You can play with up to ten friends at a time and invite as many friends as you want to join your Realm. When you set up a Realm, you pay a fee but your friends get in for free. Their servers are always online, so your friends can log on and play even when you're AWK (away from your keyboard). See **Realms** for information on how to set up your own Realm.

TO CONNECT VIA LAN:

1. Open Minecraft and create a new world or select an existing one using the fastest computer in the house. This will be the host server.
2. Once you've opened the game and are in the world, press the ESC or Escape key, then click the Open to LAN button.
3. Select Game mode. Survival is the default, but you can select Creative mode or Adventure mode. You can also select whether you want to enable cheats (commands).
4. Click Start LAN World. You'll get a message that a local game has been hosted.

5. Other players on your home network can now open Minecraft on their computers and select Multiplayer. Their computer should automatically join the game.

Consider playing with friends and family through a LAN, or local area network.

TO JOIN A PUBLIC SERVER:

1. Open Minecraft and click Play to run the game.
2. At the main title screen, click Multiplayer.
3. Click the Add Server button.
4. Type a name for the server in the Server Name box, then type the server address in the Server Address box. Typically this will be a domain name, such as mc.intercraften.org, or an IP address, such as 1.2.3.4. Then click Done to add the server to your server list.
5. To add a new server, click Add Server and enter the server details. You can then connect to the server with the Join Server button.
6. Select a server in the list, then click the Join Server button to connect.

Click on the server name to join one you've already been to or click Add Server to add a new one. There are many servers listed in this encyclopedia. Add the ones that sound fun to your server list as you read through this book and try them out. Some may require you to fill out an application first before you join.

TO SET UP A PRIVATE SERVER

You can connect with friends online even if you're not in the same house linked by a wifi connection. You can do this by setting up your own server and inviting friends to play with you on it. It's possible to set up a home server completely on your own through the Minecraft site at minecraft.net/download. Your server will only be available when your computer is on and running the program, which means you'll either have to leave it running all the time for friends to join whenever they want, or your friends can only join when you're at your computer playing as well.

Fortunately, there are many sites that make it easy to create your own server without the hassle of setup and hosting issues. Almost all sites will charge a fee to host your server for you and give you plugins. Aternos is an ad-supported hosting site that lets you host your site for free and offers lots of plugins and options to customize your gameplay and maximize your fun with friends on your own private server. Each host has a different signup process. Simply choose the host you want to use, then follow the instructions to set up your server, invite friends, and start playing.

HOW TO CHOOSE THE BEST SERVERS

With so many servers out there, it might be hard to find the best one for you. Dedicated multiplayer gamers have their favorites and log on depending on what they feel like doing that day or whom they're meeting up with. Try the ones listed throughout this book and see what you think. There's no commitment when you join a new server. If you like it, keep coming back. If not, no harm done. The servers listed in this encyclopedia are some of the most welcoming, family-friendly, fun, and reliable environments out there, but that doesn't mean there aren't plenty of others. New servers are established every day, so stay open-minded and you'll find tons of ways to improve your gaming experience. When you're looking for a multiplayer server, whitelisted servers—ones you need to be an approved user to play—are a better bet than open or greylisted servers. You should also look for a server that has moderated chats or has the ability to turn chatting off; has the amount of block protection, griefing protection, or plot protection you're comfortable with; and offers the best experience for you.

EXPERT TIPS: MULTIPLAYER MANNERS

"To help everyone feel welcome, the first thing to do is just say 'hi' or 'hello' when someone logs on. This started from day one. Back when I just played, I jumped on many servers and most of the time no one even recognized that I had logged on. This simple step over time has grown. Almost every time someone logs onto our servers, multiple players will say 'hi.' When someone new comes on, there is a special message to alert everyone and everyone welcomes that person! Some even say 'one of us.'"

—Jimmy Tassin, Omnikraft founder

A

ADDSTAR:

Addstar MC is a self-described fun survival server with a friendly player community. Log into Addstar and choose a different experience every time. Play games or mini-games and meet friends as you play. Not sure how to play? Don't sweat it. Visit http://addstar.com.au/games for video tutorials on all the basics. You can also just wander around and float up through waterfalls, Parkour around the SkyBlock survival worlds, and explore on your own. Addstar plugins include Grief Prevention, FoundDiamonds, Log Block, LWC, Craftipedia, Mini-games, LotteryPlus, ChessCraft, CasinoSlots, Citizens, and more.

Because this server is designed to be kid-friendly, all player builds and homes are protected by Grief Prevention. As an added bonus, Addstar has the ability to roll back any griefing to restore builds and property when you report it. This site features chat censoring to disable swearing and has staff monitoring the boards to provide assistance or just have a chat. Their rules include no griefing, no hacks, no trolling, no spamming, no swearing, no nagging, and no shouting (typing in all caps). Visit http://addstar.com.au to find the server information and log on.

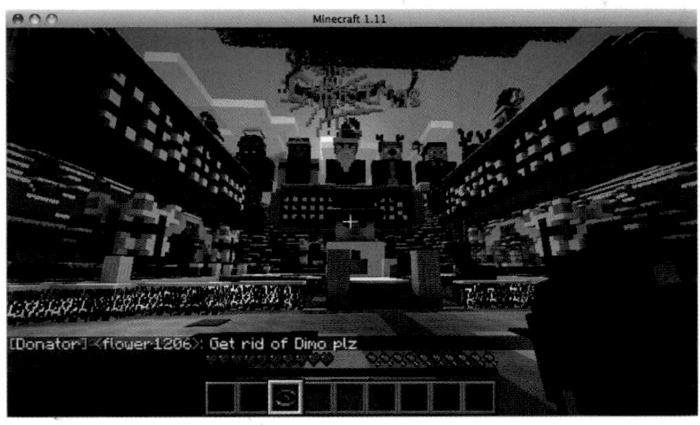

The main hall of Addstar is decorated for the holiday season. Choose your adventure from here.

You might find this Addstar banner on a list of family-friendly survival servers. Click to find out more information.

For the best color block party on the block, check out Addstar MC. This quick mini-game may be the best harmless fun you can have in multiplayer mode.

Choose from the list of servers you've already added or click Add Server on the bottom right to add a new server.

ADMIN (ADMINISTRATOR):

An admin works for the server. They help players, enforce rules, and ban players who behave badly. Also known as SAdmin or Super Admin, they set overall server rules, build the server, and create the world rules. They also monitor chat, help boards, and player behavior; ban players; resolve issues in "god mode"; and sometimes help resolve player conflicts.

ADVENTURE MODE:

In Adventure mode, servers devise a game around player-created maps. Standard Vanilla gameplay is limited to avoid destroying certain blocks that contribute to the game. In Adventure mode, you craft items; interact with mobs, item frames, and paintings; and use command blocks. *Why would I want to do that?* you may ask. Well, say you've created a really cool maze and want to challenge your friends to complete it in record time—or without having their character die a gruesome mob-related death. You don't want them to just smash through the walls and get to the end, so you create it in Adventure mode and make them walk, hop, and possibly shoot their way through whatever challenges you put in their way. Adventure mode is also perfect for Parkour and SkyBlock maps and any other PvE, or Player versus Environment world.

Minecraft: Story Mode is a graphic adventure video game by Telltale Games that allows you to choose your adventure as you play.

TIP

If you're setting up a LAN, Server, or Realm, you can switch your server to Adventure mode from any other game mode with any of the following commands:

/gamemode adventure

/gamemode a

/gamemode 2

In Minecraft: Story Mode, you can go online to solve puzzles, fight zombies, and talk to other characters to progress the story.

In Adventure mode you're free to explore and interact with the environment. Different servers offer different experiences.

You have a limited time to make your choice in some adventures.

AFK:

Typing in the command /afk during a multiplayer game tells others that you're away from your keyboard. If you are away from your keyboard for an extended period, servers may kick you off due to inactivity. This is for your own protection—you wouldn't want to come back and find zombies have invaded your home—and for the server, too.

ALLIANCE:

A great way to succeed in Multiplayer mode is to create friendships, or "alliances," with other players. Having friends in Minecraft will make mischievous and destructive players (griefers) think twice about destroying or stealing your things, and when they do, you will have backup in attacking them. You will also have backup when you come across hostile mobs. Helping players build a house or defeat a mob, as well as giving them items they may want that you don't need, is a great way to begin alliances with other players.

ANARCHY:

An Anarchy server has almost no rules, so enter at your own risk, and whatever you do, don't look like a noob (newbie who doesn't know their way around the game). It's kill or be killed, eat or be eaten, steal or be robbed in an Anarchy world. If you're okay with it, then it can be a lot of fun, but beware: Anarchy servers usually have pretty hard-core griefing and swearing, and aren't big on moderating what users do or how they behave. This PvP (Player versus Player) game is the basis of most online gameplay. Most adults feel it's NSFK (not safe for kids), so if you're a minor, you should get an adult's permission before joining.

In this Anarchy server map, there are no rules and many obstacles. Choose your allies carefully. Keep your friends close and your enemies closer.

ARCADE GAMES:

Some servers host arcade games, which can be considered different from classic or mini-games in that arcade games are much shorter, usually lasting no more than 20 minutes each. Some servers call arcade games mini-games and call classic games arcade games, but don't sweat the difference too much—just check out which ones a server has to offer and go play!

There are many different arcade games, from ones that mirror actual arcade games like air hockey and Pac-Man, to real-life games like paintball and capture the flag (also known as CTF), to ones that challenge you to complete a quest.

Some servers have specific areas on the map where you can access games. Others have you enter by waterfall, portal, compass, warp, or teleport.

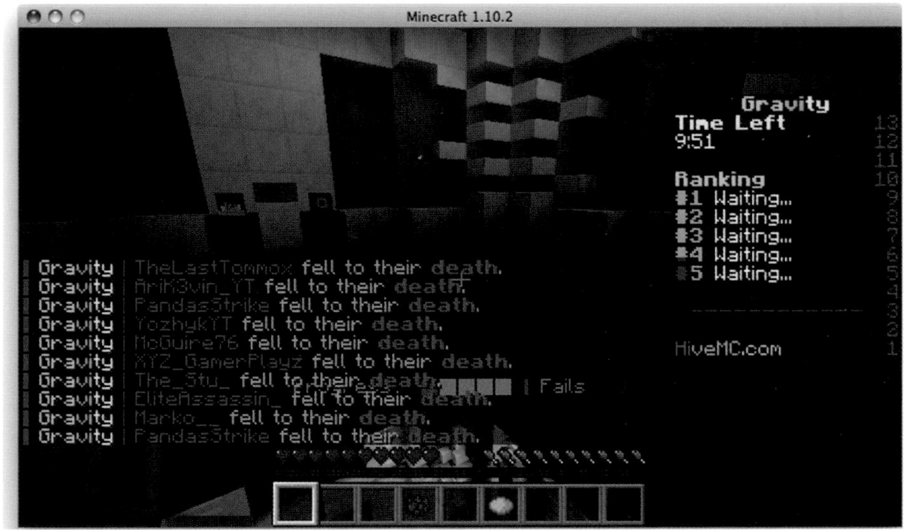

Gravity is one of many arcade games you can play in The Hive. In this game, you get to zoom around space wearing a jetpack and shooting other players with gravity guns. Don't run out of oxygen or jet fuel or you'll be a goner.

ATERNOS:

Aternos is a platform where you can host your own Minecraft server for free. Visit http://aternos.org to see it for yourself and get more information. The server is hosted on the machines of Aternos and not on your own computer. That makes it a lot easier for other players to connect to this server and it will not slow down your computer. It's also much faster and less complicated, because you only have to sign up using your email address. The email address is only used to restore your password if you forget it. After you have signed up, you can start your server with a single click. By default it will start a Vanilla Minecraft server with the latest version, so you can immediately start a Survival multiplayer session with your friends. But there are many more ways to customize your server. Aternos is a great platform to start playing around with plugins or try a modpack with your friends. All these plugins, mods, and modpacks are handpicked by the Aternos staff to ensure the best security and child safety that is possible. And if you run into any problems with your server, the Aternos support team can help.

While other platforms may charge you for their services, Aternos is a free alternative. Money from ads helps keep the platform running. (The ads are not overwhelming and do not feature anything unsafe for children.) Aternos is run by a small team of young German Minecraft players and computer specialists. It's been around since 2013 and has more than 2.5 million users from around the world.

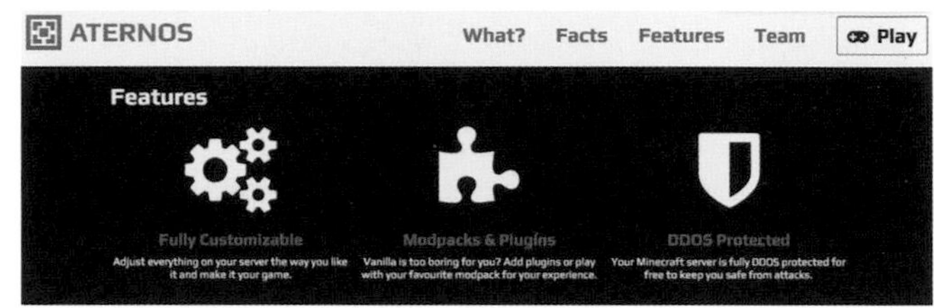

Aternos offers a lot of choices to gamers who are ready to run their own server.

Aternos servers are free to create. Once you have your own multiplayer game server, you can have more control over your gaming experience.

A WHOLE NEW WORLD (AWNW):

AWNW is a server that was started by SpaZMonKeY777 and Kaioko, who wanted to create an easy way to play Minecraft with their friends and family. The site grew so quickly that they opened the server up to more registered users. Now it's a really big gaming network that offers lots of ways to play online.

A Whole New World is a whitelist server that offers build contests and mini-events along with SkyBlock, creative and survival worlds within the world.

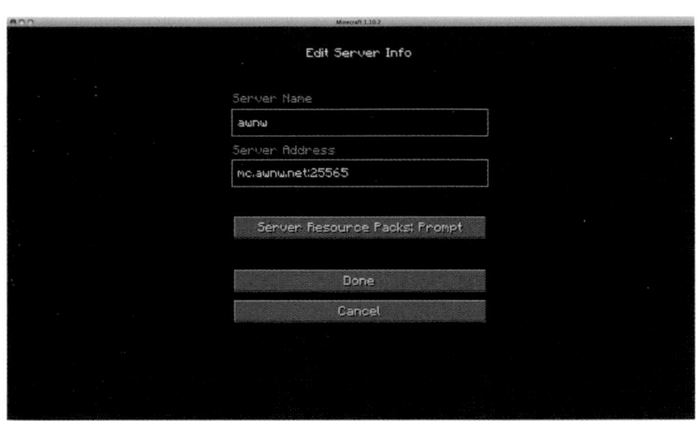

To try a new server, just type in the server name and IP address and you'll be on your way to popular multiplayer games like SkyBlock and Pixelmon.

Their servers include:

- Lobby
- Survival
- Hard mode
- SkyBlock
- Creative
- Pixelmon
- Museums

Mini-games offered:

- Mob Arena
- Block Hunt
- Paintball Arena
- Super Spleef

Part of what makes AWNW so much fun is the extra **McMMO** plugins like acrobatics, parties, and taming, which expand gameplay and give you more ways to have fun in the game. If you join AWNW, check out the additional in-game commands you can use to maximize the fun.

Visit www.awnw.net to learn more. Log in to server ID: mc.awnw.net:25565.

B

BAN:

Every server has its own set of rules. If you don't follow the rules, the server admin can ban you from playing. An admin will set a time limit for your ban—a day, a week, a month, etc.—but it's rarely permanent unless you've done something so terrible that they never want you back on their server again. If you get permanently banned or kicked off a server, your ID may get added to a "permanent ban" list, which could cause other whitelist servers not to accept you.

If someone is bullying, griefing, or teasing you, contact the moderator, admin, or whoever is supervising the server. Kid-friendly servers usually have a moderator on-chat and on-call all the time. Visit the server's website to find out which moderator is online, then type /msg (player name) (message). For example, if you are trying to tell "smod62happydude" that you've been griefed and you need help, type the following:

/msg smod62happydude
Can you please help me? I'm being bullied.

You may also want to take a screenshot of the bully in action, the text chat that resulted in your being bullied, or at least evidence of the damage that was done.

Appealing a ban

Everyone makes mistakes—players do, and admins can, too. If you are banned from a server, you can almost always contact the admin to plead your case and see if you can get the ban lifted. Here are some guidelines for appealing a ban:

- Do not use bad or nasty words when asking for an appeal.
- Please be polite and be understanding.
- Give a short, honest explanation of your side of the story. Chances are the admins know enough details to catch a lie and confirm an explanation.
- Take responsibility for your actions on the server.

Note

An admin can ban either your Minecraft username or your IP address—the computer you're using to play the game. If your username is banned, you *could* log in with a different username, but be warned: if an admin sees a banned player return under a different name, the ban could be extended.

BIOMES:

In Multiplayer mode, just as with Single-player mode, biomes are areas with different climates, mobs, and other geographical features. However, the biomes that are best for survival and success when in Single-player mode are not the best when playing in Multiplayer mode. The best biomes for Multiplayer mode are Plains, Savanna, and Extreme Hills. The open spaces of the Savanna and Plains Biomes make it harder to collide with the "territories" of other players. Avoid the Forest and Mushroom Island Biomes when playing in Multiplayer mode. Trees attract a vast number of players, making the Forest and Jungle Biomes crowded and full of griefers who will set fires and steal items from houses. The isolation of the Mushroom Island Biome makes it crowded as well.

You can enjoy extra space from competitors and untapped resources in the wide-open Plains Biome.

BLOCK HUNT:

Block Hunt, also known as Prop Hunt or Hide and Seek, is a game mode on Minecraft where you get to *be* a prop like a fence, a creeper, or another everyday object and hide in plain sight, hoping your opponents don't find you. Creepy or fun? You decide!

When you're playing hide and seek, it can sometimes help to camouflage yourself—like hiding as a wooden block up against a tree.

BLOCKS VS. ZOMBIES:

If you like Plants vs. Zombies, you'll love Blocks vs. Zombies! It's a Bukkit plugin that you can install on your own server to play against your friends.

How to play: Survive an onslaught of zombies for 20 minutes and you win this mini-game. The intensity builds as you begin shooting arrows at a slow but steady trickle of zombies and use your gold and points to purchase barriers for added protection. Upgrade your weapons and use cannons and traps to take down more zombies at once. This game offers an instruction manual to guide newbies through the rules of the game.

TIP

Watch out for invisible zombies!

You can easily search online to see which whitelisted servers offer this game. There are plenty to choose from. Select the one that has a lot of regular players to increase your chances of a good pickup game when you want it.

Blocks vs. Zombies uses command blocks to take your love of the Plants vs. Zombies app to a whole new level.

BUKKIT:

Bukkit/CraftBukkit is a server software that can be used with plugins. Officially, the program behind it is called Bukkit and the actual usable server software is called CraftBukkit, but Bukkit is often used for the server software. Bukkit was created by team members of the hMod, one of the first Minecraft server modifications. In 2014, Bukkit experienced a huge crisis, which led to the end of the project. Today, Bukkit is maintained by the Spigot team.

C

CAPTURE THE FLAG, OR CTF:

Capture the Flag is a multiplayer game where two or more teams each try to capture an item—usually a flag—from the enemy base and bring it to their own base while also guarding their own flag.

Join this multiplayer showdown if you like the idea of infiltrating your enemy's base where players are guarding a very precious item. From the instant you join the game you'll be teleported into an ongoing game and placed on the team that needs you most. Your entire head will change to red or blue to match your teammates' and you'll be on your way to helping your team protect the coveted flag or hunt down the enemy.

How do you know who has the flag in his or her grasp? Follow the lightning flashes and the player who's running around in a cloud of fiery sparks!

TIP

Want to be rewarded for quick-footed victory? Join the "Monk" class if speed is your strength.

Capture the Flag is a fun, fast-paced game. It takes a few tries to get the hang of it. As soon as you join a game, find your flag and see if it needs defending and find a good, high hiding place to get a sense of the arena and your opponents' locations.

CHAT:

Multiplayer mode has a built-in text chat feature where players can type messages to each other that appear at the bottom of the screen. For some players, chat is the reason they play online. And for some parents and teachers, it's a reason to keep kids off servers. Even with strict server rules, without filters, text messages can get inappropriate. Players find ways around filters that don't let you use swear words, for one thing. And just like in an unsupervised playground, there are bullies and people who can get pretty mean. Many servers have full-time moderators who watch what goes on, step in when there's a problem, and help resolve conflicts. On most servers, regular players watch each other's backs and stand up for each other if they see a problem.

There are ways to disable certain chat features when you're online. For example, you can turn off chat on your computer, ignore players who are bothering you using the /ignore command, only join servers that have full-time supervision, or join servers that block chat entirely.

Rookie players can use chat to ask more experienced players important questions or just to joke around with other players and have fun.

To turn off chat:

1. Hit Escape to bring up the Settings menu.
2. Click on Options.
3. On the Options screen, select Multiplayer Settings.
4. Select Chat Shown and set it to either show Commands Only or just be hidden. With chat hidden, new chat messages from other players won't show up and you won't be able to chat. Keeping commands visible will let you still type commands, which are necessary for some servers.

TIP

Someone bugging you but you don't want one bad apple to ruin the whole bunch? Bring up the Command screen and type /ignore, then the user's name to block only those comments.

Click Multiplayer Settings to change what types of chat messages show onscreen as you play.

CLAIMS:

Some servers, like **Towncraft** and **Cubeville**, offer players the ability to claim a parcel of land that only they can play on. These servers usually use a plugin called Grief Prevention to protect land claims. It's also called Free Build on servers like **MC Magic**. Claiming land with Grief Prevention is easy. Simply set up a chest in the center of your house, then use a golden shovel to define the outside corners of the land you want to claim. You can also type "how do I claim land?" in the game to get a step-by-step tutorial.

On Towncraft, for example, you automatically receive 100 blocks of protection when you first log in and you earn additional blocks for every hour you spend on their server. You can also buy blocks with "sponge" that you get in the game from mobs and contests.

Some servers make you work to earn virtual money in order to afford your own plot of land.

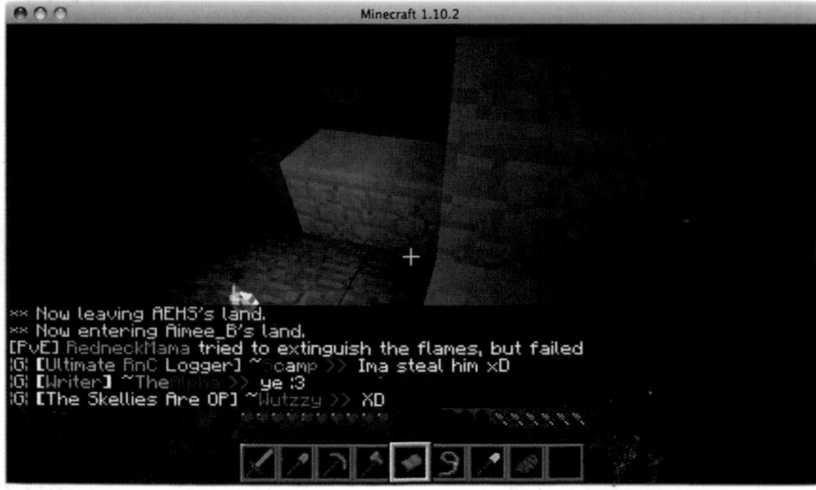

Some servers offer claims where you can build your own homestead. In Ranchcraft, you're welcome to visit other players' ranches, spend the night, and even rent their horses if you don't have one of your own.

C

CLOSED SERVER:

Closed servers are servers that are not open for the public, so not everyone can join and play on these servers. This can be a server where some friends are enjoying their private survival experience or a server that has age restrictions. Closed servers often use a **whitelist** or sometimes even a **greylist** to prevent unwanted players from joining the server.

COMMANDS:

You may rarely use server commands when you're playing in Single-player mode on your home computer or you may use them a lot

SERVER COMMANDS

Try a few of these commands in Multiplayer mode to liven up the experience and keep things interesting. Not all of these commands will work on all servers. For a full list of available game commands, type in /help.

/lobby or /leave lets you leave a multiplayer game and go back to choose another.

/whisper<player name><message> lets you send a message to a specific friend and no one else.

/give<player><item>[amount][datavalue] lets you give an item to another player. (Data value refers to things such as the color of the item if it is something like wool.)

/tp<player><player2> lets you teleport yourself to another player by using the command.

/kill[player] lets you deliver 1000 void damage to an opposing player. If you forget to put in the name of the player, though, you will accidentally kill yourself, so be careful!

/list lets you view which players are online.

/sethome sets your home point to where you're currently standing.

/home teleports you home.
/setspawn sets your current location as your spawn point.

/tp X Y Z teleports you to a specific place where X, Y, and Z are the coordinates.

when cheats are enabled. In fact, some people even refer to commands as cheats!

In multiplayer worlds, many servers rely on commands for important gameplay features. To start a command, press T on your keyboard or type the / (slash) key, then enter the command name. You may have to include extra text with additional direction as well. Some servers have unique commands that are easy enough to grasp and master. If you're uncertain which commands are available, most servers will let you scroll through a list of available commands when you type / and keep pressing Tab.

COPS AND ROBBERS:

In this mini-game, one player is the cop or policeman. He or she tells everyone else—the robbers—what to do. They must obey or be punished. While they are following the cop's rules, they must find a way to escape unnoticed.

Be the law or be the lawbreaker in a game of cops and robbers. Cops and Robbers is also known as Prison or Jail.

CRAFTBUKKIT:

A CraftBukkit or Bukkit server is the opposite of a Vanilla server. Vanilla is a non-modded version of Minecraft, and CraftBukkit allows for mods and plugins that expand gameplay and let you do more things. Game expansion is possible because Minecraft was built on an open platform called Sandbox that allows anyone to add new features to the program to change the way the game is played. CraftBukkit is the program you download that lets these plugins work with the official Minecraft server when you are running Minecraft in Single-player mode on your home computer, hosting a LAN networked game, or hosting a Minecraft server. You do not need to download CraftBukkit if you are joining another server in progress or want to play the Vanilla version of the game.

CRAZYPIG:

CrazyPig is a family-friendly Minecraft multiplayer server with adult admins and a staff dedicated to fun and online safety. The site disables swearing, offers in-game chat that can be switched on or off, and has Griefing Protection. The site map includes:

CrazyPig offers special events to make holidays merry and bright.

- A Lobby where you can enter all the other worlds
- Cambria, a hard mode Survival mode
- Insania, an extra-hard Survival mode
- Games, a mini-games world
- Atlantica, an easy mode Survival mode for new players
- Plots, a creative world where players are assigned a claim where they can build whatever they want

Visit http://crazypig.enjin.com to learn more. Log in at server IP play.crazypig.net.

CREATIVE MODE:

In Creative mode, you have an infinite number of blocks to build with, you never take damage, you never get hungry, all mobs are neutral, and you can fly. Gameplay on a creative server is centered on building and creating interactive experiences, such as theme parks, town communities, and construction projects. Minecraft Middle Earth is one example of a Creative mode server. It aims to recreate the entire world from J.R.R. Tolkien's *Lord of the*

Rings books and recruits builders and project managers to help build the world one tree and block at a time.

CUBECRAFT:

Founded in 2013, CubeCraft is one of the world's largest Minecraft networks, with more than 100,000 players logging on to their servers every day and up to 30,000 players online at one time. The site hosts unique games like SkyWars, Tower Defence, Lucky Islands, MinerWare, and EggWars! The upside is that there are loads of unique solo player and team player games and you can always find a game in progress with lots of players on at once. The

There are many places to explore in the world of CubeCraft.

This is the main hall of CubeCraft.

CubeCraft has different channels so you can chat within the game or world you're in or choose a specific channel for server-wide chat.

downside is that this server is not whitelisted—anyone can join—but there are server admins who pay close attention and will ban players who don't follow the rules. While CubeCraft is free, some of the plugins have to be purchased online. Visit www.cubecraft.net to learn more. Log in to server ID: play.cubecraftgames.net.

CUBEVILLE:

Cubeville is a big world with many different areas, so there should be something fun for everyone. You spawn in a big central city with a large map on the wall. You can't scroll to see the map, but it does give you an idea of just how big the world is. Take the tutorial when you arrive—it's really hard to get around unless you take the time.

There are smaller towns and settlements dotted across the world, and you can visit them through the skyway, a transport system that can take you all the way to the outer edges of the map. Hop on and see where it takes you!

Cubeville has a money system with quests to earn cash. You can spend that cash at automated shops. And when you're ready to set up your own little corner of the world, there is chest protection and land claiming, so you'll always have a place to hang your sword when you visit.

You don't need to apply to join—just enter cubeville.org into your Minecraft client—but the server is very family-friendly with grown-up moderators who really want to help players have fun.

What Cubeville doesn't have:

- PvP
- Swearing
- Age limits

What Cubeville does have:

- Friendly moderators
- Supervised play
- A safe zone in the main city where monsters can't spawn, even at night
- Basic free supplies

TIP

Are you afraid of the dark? There's no sleeping in Multiplayer mode, and monsters do spawn at night. If you want to avoid them, spend the night in the well-lit main city. It's a safe zone and a great place to see who else is online while you wait until sunrise.

Note:

While Cubeville is free, special swag is awarded to players who donate money to fund the server and keep it running. Onetime donors get a dollar sign next to their name, and ongoing donors get to wear blocks on their heads! Servers are not able to reward donors with anything that provides an in-game advantage. Visit www.cubeville.org to learn more. Log in to server ID: cubeville.org.

CUSTOM SERVER:

If you've ever wanted to be the master of your own domain, you can do it in Minecraft. It's easy to set up a server and you can even do it for free. Enjin is one of a handful of sites that lets you create your own Minecraft server and customize it, to a point, without paying a cent. If your server becomes successful and you are willing and able to pay a monthly fee, you can add features to make gameplay more exciting and site management easier. There are lots of

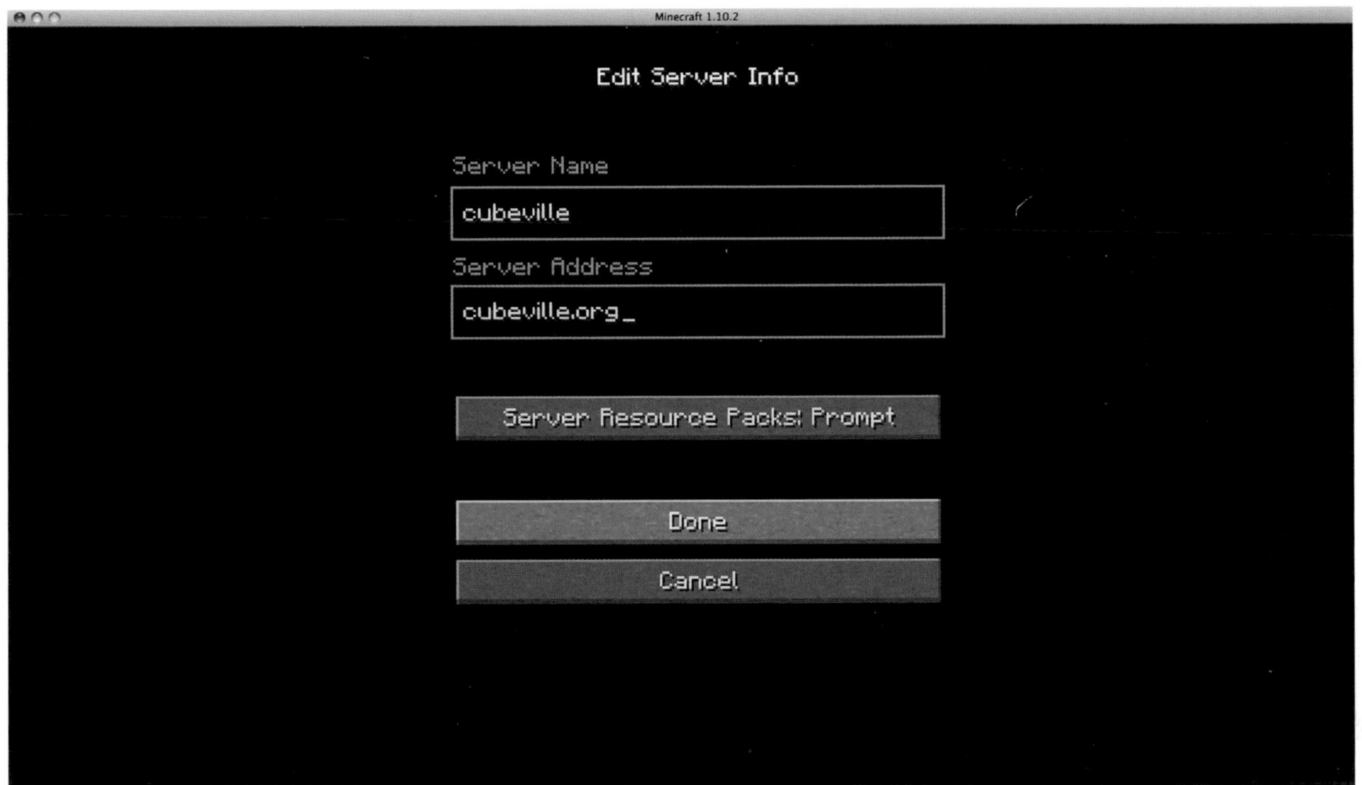

You can join Cubeville without a whitelist. Just type in the server address, log on and start playing.

benefits to joining a network to help you run your site:

- They make it easy to download and plug in what you need.
- You can get added features like voice or text chat.
- Once you join, your site will instantly be promoted on the server.
- You can advertise that you're looking for players or moderators to help you run the site.
- You can put in help tickets to get support if something is not working correctly.
- Most hosts will help you advertise on your social media channels. If you have lots of Instagram followers, for example, that's a huge bonus.

CYCLONE NETWORK:

A popular server, Cyclone Network is bound to have at least a few dozen players online at any given time during normal gaming hours. Cyclone offers games, servers, and mini-games, including OPPrison, Prison, Factions, SkyBlock, and Skywars. Visit www.cyclonenetwork.org to learn more. Log in to server ID: MC.cyclonenw.org.

This dynamic banner on a server list site gives you an idea of how many players are on the Cyclone Network at any given time.

In a Prison game, you need to follow the guards' directions or get a time out.

+5 blood!
[VampireZ]: FanKonar was killed by osan15678
vampire!

Round III 00:46
53
s 24
es 10
ors 7
nd became a

DEFENSE:

There are three different types of physical defenses in a Minecraft multiplayer server: Active, Passive, and Hybrid. Active defenses are actions you take to destroy a threat to your home or base. Active defenses include using dispensers to set traps for mobs and enemy players, setting up minefields around your base with TNT, and setting up TNT canons on top of your base. Passive defenses are actions you can take to stop a potential threat before it becomes a real threat. These actions are not deadly to mobs or other players, but slow them down. These include confusing cobwebs, mazes of block walls, and water moats surrounding your base. Hybrid defenses are actions you can take that are a combination of active and passive. This can include mazes of block walls with lava behind them to destroy a threat when it tries to break through a wall, moats of lava around your base, and cactus plants set up around or inside your base.

You'll need a plan of defense when you find yourself confronted with a hostile mob like this baby zombie. Active, passive, and hybrid approaches to defense will all help you survive longer.

nicahdg
100
Glass
nicahdg
50
Coal
nicahdg
100
Glass
nicahdg
50
Jungle Log
nicahdg
100
Glass
nicahdg
50
Birch Log
nicahdg
100
Sandstone
nicahdg
50
Redwood Log
nicahdg
50
Glowstone
nicahdg
50
Log

E

ECONOMY:

An economy server, or a server that features an economy, has a system set up where players can earn currency by doing tasks or selling goods. They use the currency to hire labor so they can build a large structure, buy food or rare materials, and purchase products made by someone else, such as weapons or tools.

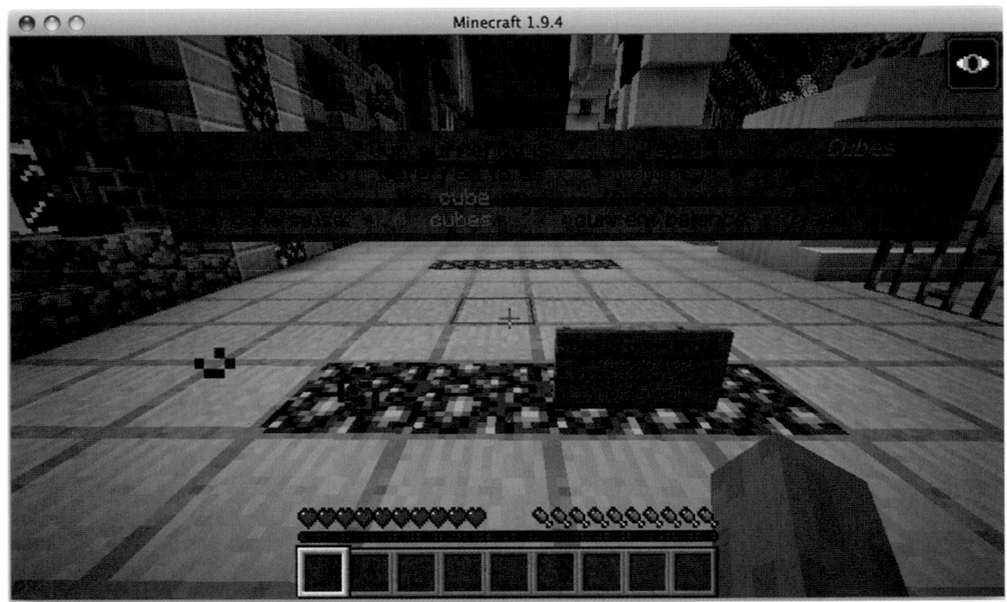

CubeCraft is one site that offers a full working economy. Read the signs as you walk through the tutorial to learn all the details.

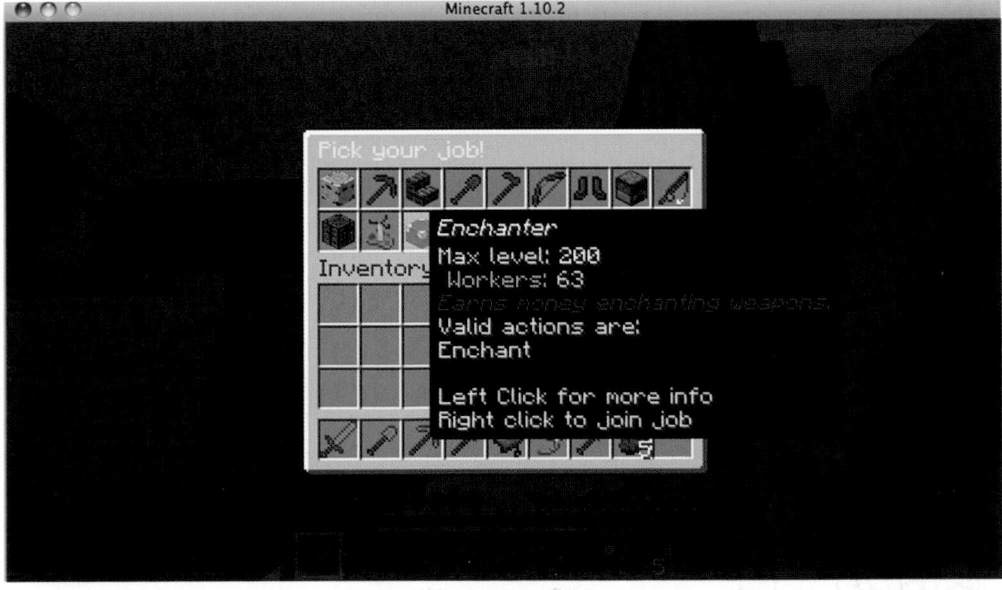

RanchNCraft is one server that features an economy.

One economy server you can try is Famcraft, where you can work to earn money, buy and sell items and services, and negotiate prices. It's like playing house, or store, or business mogul. Some economy servers invite you to get a job, craft items for sale, mine for items, or complete tasks to earn currency that will get you all sorts of cool perks. Use your earnings to buy items from other players or get extras from the server gods like more land, superpowers, or entry into restricted games or areas. It's like being an adult, but a lot more fun.

An example of a working economy on the Famcraft server.

ENJIN.COM:

Enjin is a hosting company that makes it easy to create your own Minecraft server. They provide the tools, plugins, and information needed to set up a social gaming network, recruit friends, and more. Enjin hosts most of your favorite MC servers like Mineplex, AWNW, and Potterworld. Visit the Enjin.com website for a list of Enjin servers in order of their popularity.

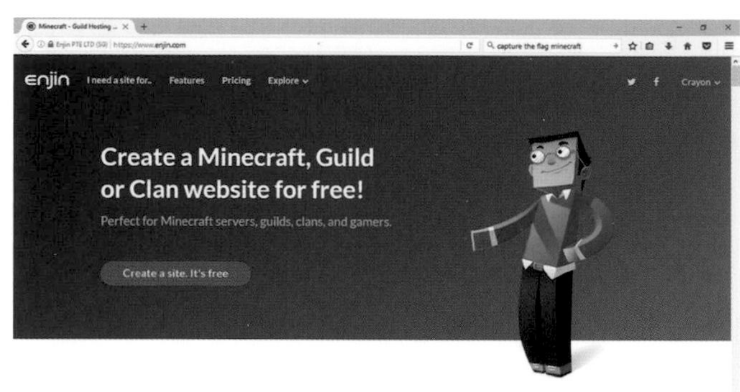

You have many options to take your gaming to the next level and lead your own server.

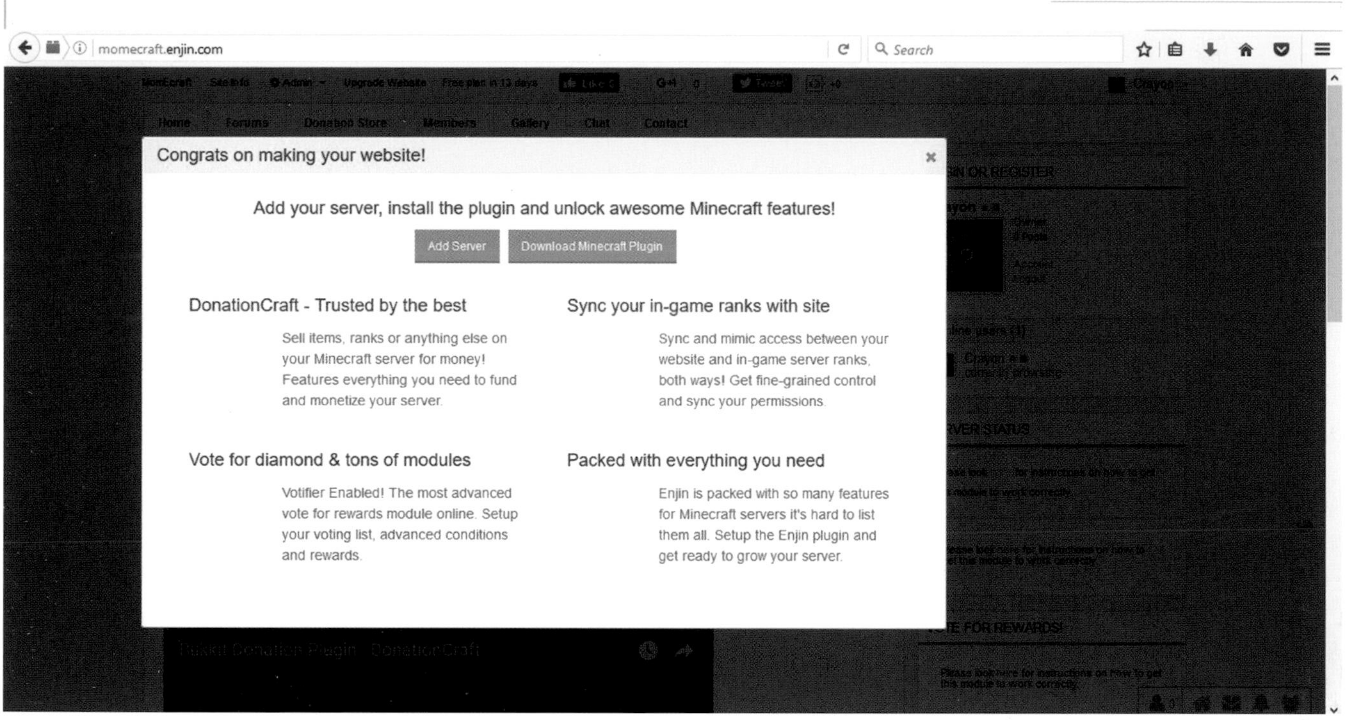

There are many different ways to grow and develop your server.

ESRB:

The ESRB rating for Minecraft is E for Everyone 10+ for fantasy violence. This rating, however, applies only to Single-player mode. Once you start to interact with other players, online interactions are not rated by the ESRB. Minecraft is listed in the ESRB database as a puzzle-adventure game where players mine pixilated landscapes to harvest cubes, play in an open world environment, craft weapons, defend themselves against monsters, and use dynamite to fend off hostile mobs and mine the land for resources.

EVOLVEHQ:

EvolveHQ is a social network and collaboration toolset for PC gamers, including Minecraft players. They make it easy for gamers to connect, coordinate, and play games online with an app that members install on their PCs. EvolveHQ features chat and voice communication tools, a virtual LAN, matchmaker for multiplayer games like Minecraft, screen and video capture, and video streaming tools all in one app that goes with you in-game. This means that not only can you play Minecraft online with friends, but you can also run video-capture to create YouTube videos of your amazing builds and daring zombie-fighting deeds, including voice-overs, just like your favorite Minecraft YouTubers! Learn more and sign up for an account at www.evolvehq.com.

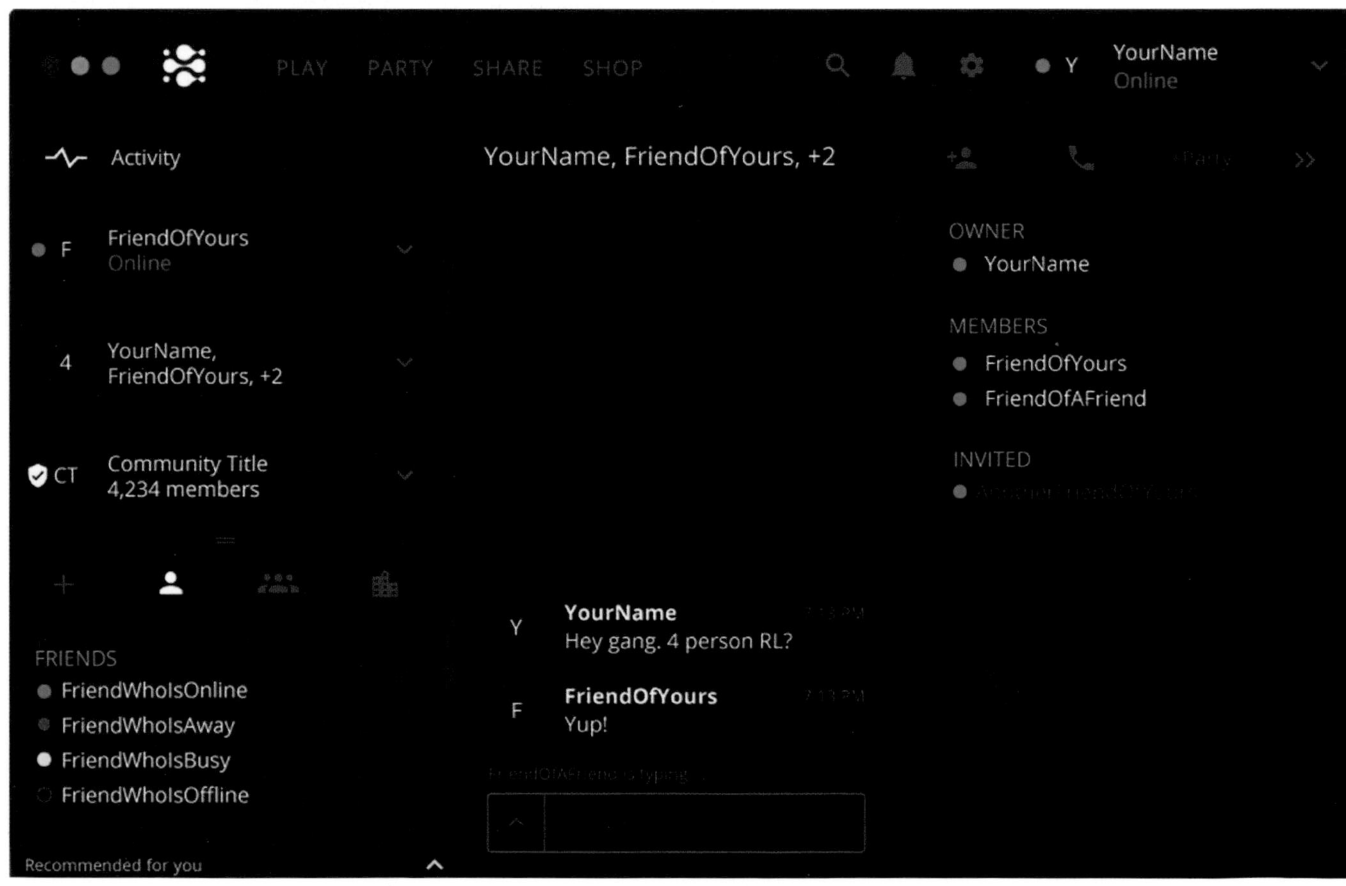

Have a party with friends around the block or around the world.

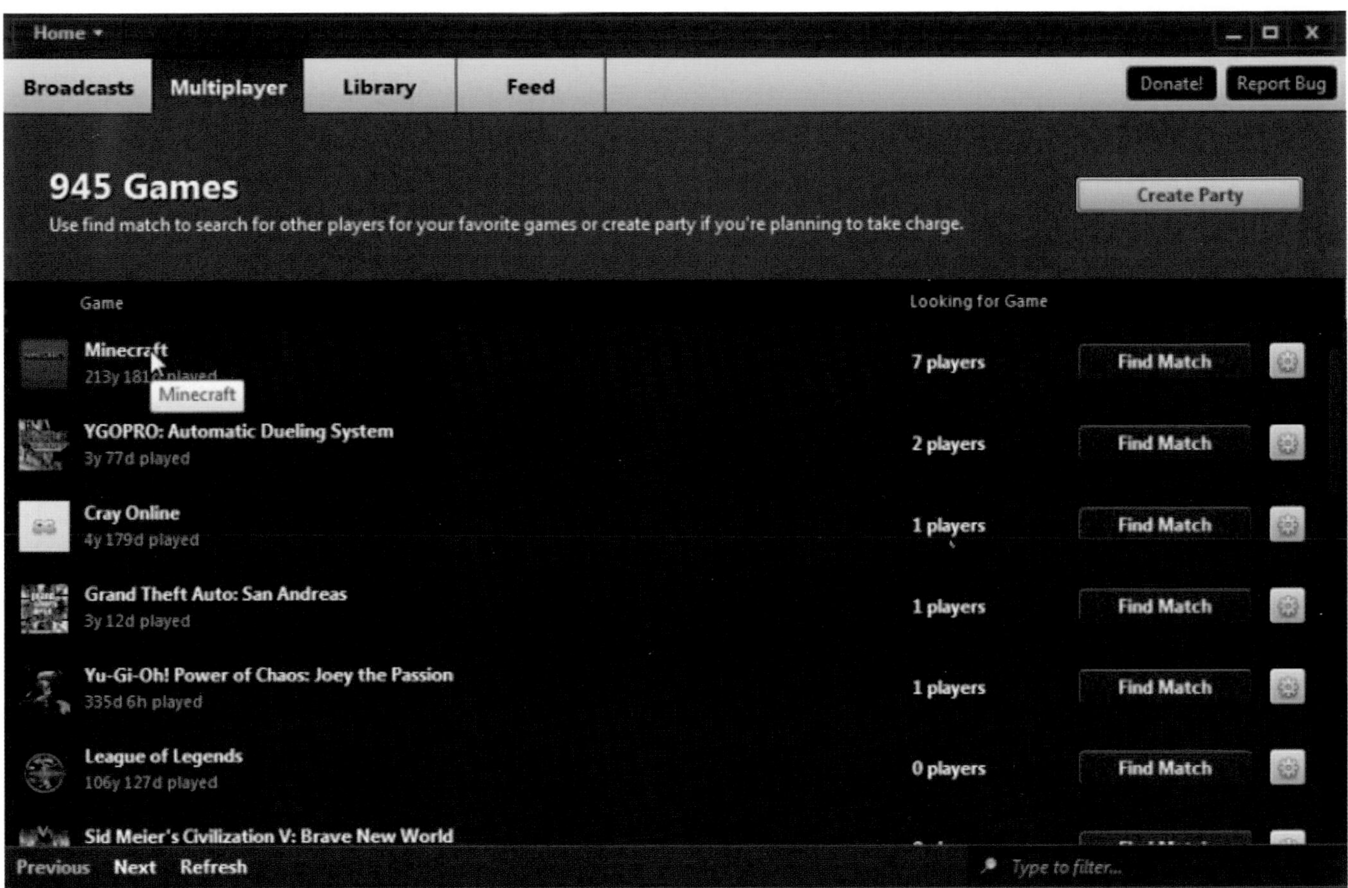

Never play alone again. Evolve's matchmaker lets you know when your friends are online and helps you set up gaming parties for multiple games at a time.

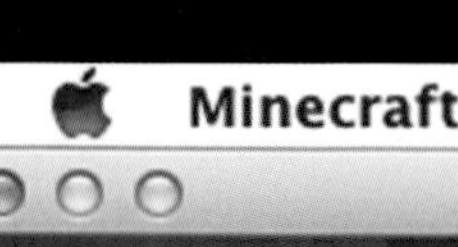
Minecraft
pvpkim was uncovered and killed by

F

FACTIONS:

Factions are a type of PvP game that consists of an epic PvP Battleground. Here, players can create factions and guilds to claim territory, make alliances, and declare war on enemies. Win a war to claim enemy territory and try to take over the world one faction at a time. Uberminecraft and GuildCraft are two of the more popular Factions servers.

In the Minecraft Faction server, you can team up with friends or join a faction already in progress.

There are many maps to choose from. Each map provides a different experience in a factions game.

This fire-filled user-created factions map is a perfect arena for a Factions game where players team up in a fight to the finish.

FALLOUT ATLANTA:

Enter a wasteland after a nuclear apocalypse and use your survival skills in Fallout Atlanta. Try your luck on your own against radiation and ghouls in a sprawling wasteland with shells of buildings to scavenge through, vaults to explore, and a series of quests to complete. You can also join a Factions game where you team up to fight to the death over resources. Log in at IP fallout.gromgaming.net.

Enter prison quest and follow the flares as the guards direct you in Fallout Atlanta.

FAMCRAFT:

Famcraft is a free-to-use server that lets you practice your skills earning money and negotiating prices while you enjoy nonstop gaming fun. Part of the fun is selecting jobs to earn "Famcoins"—in-game money—and claim land. But the most exciting areas are the carnival, a sports stadium that offers PvP gaming, mazes, and other attractions.

Famcraft has been around for a few years now and it's a solid, well-established community where you're bound to see players online at all times. That's not always the case with some servers—you could easily log on and enter a ghost town where you're the only player online. Although it used to be an open server, there is now a whitelist to join. According to the Famcraft website, this status is subject to change, so don't be surprised if you can log in without joining the whitelist first at some point.

TIP

As soon as you log on, read the rules and a moderator will almost always offer you a guided tour. You can also take the self-guided tour by using the command /warp tour, which will fly you around to see all the rules and signs. The most important information you'll learn in the tour is how to head out into the wilderness to begin playing.

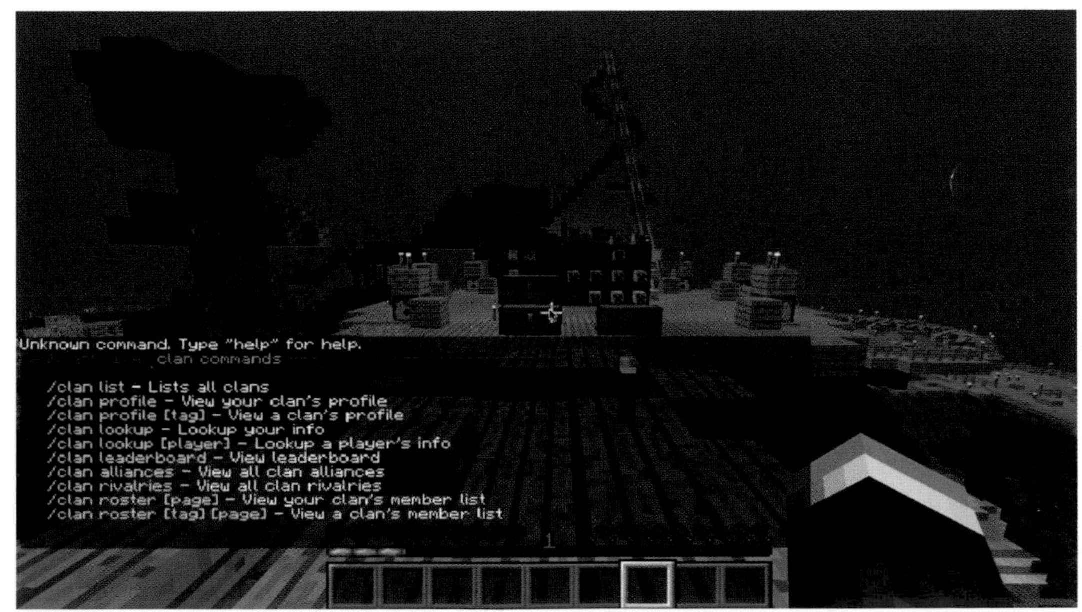

You can join a clan in Famcraft. Unsure of what command to use or what to do next? Type /help.

Rain or shine, there's a big, bright, beautiful world to explore in Famcraft.

A SERVER WITH PERKS

"Famcraft has some extra touches that give the server its own unique, community feel. For example, there are a large number of clans that you can join to work on projects together, and there are also lots of giant player statues to show appreciation for helpful players on the server. The server staff also regularly stream family-friendly music with Mixlr, which really adds an element of fun to the gameplay. They even host dance parties in a fantastic dance area within the world!"
—Matt Doyle, Brightpips.com

If you're up for a completely different challenge, you can log in with the FTB (Feed the Beast) modpack. According to the Famcraft website, there are mods for almost anything you can imagine: machines and power, magic, outer space travel, and breeding bees and trees . . . Famcraft stretches the limits of the infinite possibilities of the game!

TIP

If you're visiting the FTB server, you'll need to load 166 mods; it will take a while, so be patient. It's worth the wait!

However you play, Famcraft staff are helpful, patient, and at your service to make sure everyone gets the most out of their server.

Visit www.famcraft.com to learn more. Log in to the FeedTheBeast server ID at ftb.famcraft.com (you'll need the Private Pack Code: "famcraft") and log in to the Vanilla Survival server at survival.famcraft.com.

A survival map in Famcraft.

FTB, OR FEED THE BEAST:

Feed the Beast is a collection of server and client mods that are bundled together to provide a map, a challenge, and the tools to tackle it. These mods come in different resource packs that provide maps, themes, magic, and other modifications that basically change the beast you need to feed, the environment you are in, and the challenges you need to overcome to achieve the goal of the Feed the Beast game. FTB is featured on many different servers, including Famcraft.

To play, you'll need to visit the site you want to play on and follow the instructions to download the FTB Mod Launcher for that specific site. You don't need to go to a Feed the Beast website because each server offers a different customized FTB mod pack. Only download the pack if the server requires it, and ask an adult before you download anything to your computer.

Add the Feed the Beast mod for even more gameplay options.

FARM HUNT:

This hide-and-seek mini-game is a fantastic showdown between hunters and animals. If you enter the game as a hunter, your mission is to roam around looking for other players who are expertly disguised as animals. How can you tell which animals are actually your opponents in disguise? If they move and run, it's time to spring into action and attack them. If you enter the game as an animal, it's up to you to stay concealed from the hunters. Keep a low profile longer than everyone else and you win!

These Farm Hunt pigs may look innocent, but if they start to run, then you know you've got to hunt them down.

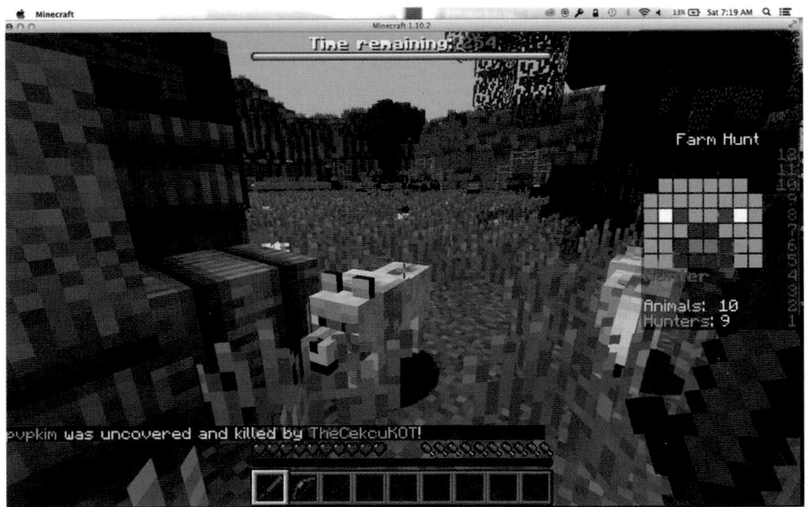

In Farm Hunt, you have to determine whether this pair of wolves is suspicious or not. They could be your opponents in disguise!

G
18

GAMES:

Multiplayer mode gives you a chance to gamify (make a game out of) your Minecraft adventure. You can play with other players on the same team, or against other players in either a Factions game where you team up or a Player versus Player mode where it's every player for him- or herself. Arcade-style games take the least amount of time to play. Mini-games take slightly longer. Some popular games are Capture the Flag, Prison Break, and Factions.

What's great about Minecraft is that whatever you're in the mood to do, there's a server where you can do it! Some games, like maze games, take only a few minutes, while others, like Capture the Flag, have a set time limit of 5 to 15 minutes. Still more, like Pixelmon, have you following an extensive storyline that takes months or even years to complete.

GREYLIST:

A greylist is based on the idea of a **whitelist** to restrict the access to a server to some selected players. Here, everyone is allowed to join the server, even if they are not on the greylist. But they are not allowed to do some essential things, like building or chatting, for example. The exact permissions for the non-greylisted players may differ from server to server. Only greylisted players have full access to the server and are allowed to build and chat. The advantage of a greylist is that players can have a look at the server before they decide to join or apply for the full access version. Greylists are not a basic part of the server software and have to be implemented with a plugin.

GRIEF PROTECTION:

Some sites install Grief Protection mods that automatically kick off, ban, or warn players who are caught destroying another player's builds. On almost all servers, griefing is prohibited, but just prohibiting it will not stop players from griefing—there are always bad players who try to destroy the game for others. Fortunately, some servers install mods that block griefing, making it impossible for the player to build/destroy in certain areas. They can also automatically keep track of every change a player does and roll the griefing back when it happens. Most servers do both. Admins can limit areas with a plugin like **WorldGuard** and assign private areas to players with a plot plugin. And they can set up a plugin that can save every block change in a database. After that, they can easily look up any change on the server to find out who has destroyed a building, for example, undo the changes, and ban the player.

GRIEFER:

A person who intentionally destroys someone else's things in Multiplayer mode.

GRIEFING:

Griefing is any action that destroys something somebody else has created. It can be as harmless as a reversible practical joke or as harmful as destroying another player's hard work. The most common meaning of *griefing* is the purposeful destruction of someone else's buildings by breaking the blocks, placing unwanted blocks, flooding the building, or blowing it up. But griefing also includes stealing and annoyance. Different sites have different griefing policies. If you don't want people messing with your stuff, check a server's policies ahead of time to see how griefing is handled. Some servers have enabled a Grief Protection plugin to automatically prevent all forms of grief. Naturally, it is prohibited to grief on nearly any server and will lead to a permanent exclusion from that server.

TIP

A clever way to help prevent other players from griefing your house is to set up a decoy house nearby and grief it yourself! Leave empty, open chests inside it and inside your "real" houses and camps so that players looking to grief you are fooled, thinking your building(s) have already been stolen from.

Flooding someone's house with lava is a form of griefing.

SERVER OPERATORS TAKE GRIEFING SERIOUSLY

"We have a plugin called CoreProtect that tracks changes in the world at a block level. It says who did what and when. It makes it easy for us to piece the picture together when someone griefed, stole, or x-rayed. It also allows us to rollback the changes to how they were before. There are other plugins that do the same, such as LogBlock and Prism."
—JimmyTassin, Omnikraft founder

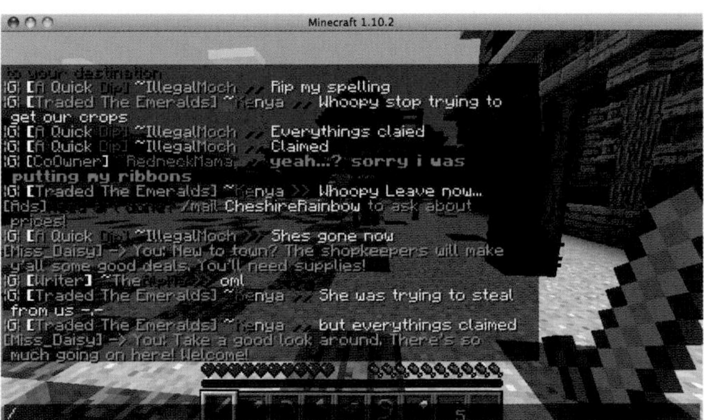

If someone is bothering you, you can report it over IRC chat in the game. On Ranch N Craft, player Kenya was being griefed by Whoopy. Kenya let Whoopy know that stealing crops is not acceptable behavior on the server.

Examples of Griefing:

- Flooding a building or farm area with lava or water
- Leaving signs or rewriting existing ones
- Locking chests or doors to prevent creators from accessing their belongings
- Destroying or rebuilding anything a player has built
- Killing farm animals or destroying farms
- Leading hostile mobs into a player's territory to destroy the player or the player's items
- Stealing items that clearly belong to another player
- Hacking or using illegal mods like flying or ore detection to gain an unfair advantage
- Harming another player on purpose if they have not agreed to PvP combat. This could include using traps, placing sand over someone's head, drowning them in water or lava, and luring mobs to kill them.
- Using a fake account to impersonate another player or post advertisements

Minecr
Ranks, Boosters, Mystery Boxes
PLAY
Blitzhunter10

1.10.2

more! ➤ STORE.HYPIXEL.NET

H

HACKS:

A hack is a modification that gives a player an unfair advantage. Some examples are speeding up travel or gameplay; banning moderators; and using infinite moves such as sneaking, flying, or remaining invisible. Hacking is a form of griefing. Report any suspected hacks to moderators. A good moderator will warn and eventually ban players for hacking behavior.

HIVE:

Adopt a PocketPet, wear a Hub Hat, and ride a mount in this super-creative, wacked-out land filled with fun and adventure. The Hive is a very popular server offering several unique gameplay options. You can perform experiments in The Lab, where you join a team of twelve players to perform three randomly generated "experiments" (which are really games) assigned by villager-scientist Dr. Zuk. You're rewarded Atoms—the local currency—based on how you play. All players on the team with the most Atoms win an Enchanted Crystal.

If mini-games aren't your thing, head over to Survival Games, where you can team up with up to three other players in a twenty-four-person traditional survival game on one of several unique maps. As in most survival games, you spawn on a map with nothing in your possession and you have one goal: to be

In the Hive, select the compass on the bottom left of the menu bar, then right click to select the game you want to play.

the last player alive. Find supply crates filled with weapons and food, form alliances, and do what you can to survive.

If you're up for a party, head over to the Hive Block Party, where you can vote for a song and play a combination of musical chairs, freeze dance, and Twister. When the music starts, join other players as you jump and dance around the dance floor. Pay attention to the bar at the top. When it announces a color, head to the nearest block of that color and stand on it. Anyone not standing on that color when the timer goes off gets dropped off the dance floor.

Other exciting game options are Trouble in Mineville, The Herobrine, Hide and Seek, Splegg, and Cowboys and Indians. Visit Hive MC to watch videos and learn the rules before you play.

The Hive has a team of more than a hundred moderators to make sure chat stays family-friendly and that people are treated in a respectful, welcoming way. It's free to play, but the site offers premium membership passes that will grant you extras, like lucky crates, pets, mounts to ride, premium items, and a chance to reset your stats and erase your early game scores so it's like your first few noob games never happened. Visit https://forum.hivemc.com to learn more.

HONOR RULES:

While breaking some rules will get you banned or kicked off a server, honor rules don't incur any punishment if you break them. Honor rules technically make it easy to cheat, but you're on your honor to do the right thing. It helps to play games with honor rules with a group of friends you trust!

HUNGER GAMES:

See Survival Games.

HYPIXEL:

Hypixel is a server built around mini-games. If you like playing games and solving puzzles, Hypixel is for you! The most popular games on the network are Build Battle, Skywars, Blitz Survival Games, Walls, and special Parkour maps. In Walls, you are dropped onto a map with no inventory and only 15 minutes to prepare for battle. Walls between you and your opponent are raised so you cannot see how they are preparing to defend themselves and attack you. Once the walls are lowered, it's a PvP struggle for survival.

Hypixel is most famous for its incredibly cool and completely uniquely designed maps.

It started out as a YouTube channel making Minecraft Adventure Maps, and now Hypixel is one of the largest Minecraft Server Networks in the world.

Hypixel is also pretty advanced in rooting out cheaters, so play this game strictly by the rules! They have a new, sophisticated detection system called Watchdog that scours the data on players to detect anyone who might be a hacker.

Visit https://hypixel.net to learn more about this server. Log in to server ID: server.hypixel.net.

Hypixel offers several mini-games, including a Kit PvP game where you choose your kit and try to survive.

Even a simple racing game can be fun on a busy server like Hypixel, where you're always sure to find someone to play with—or against!

tercraften

Welcome to the Train Station! This is your way

to get from place to place on Intercraften

pick one of the many worlds we have.

To come back to the Train Station from a world,

Trusted Antman0426: Andykara2003 d
hen the word
Apprentice Andykara2003: kk
ember artemis622: stuff upstairs too

0:30 / 2:05

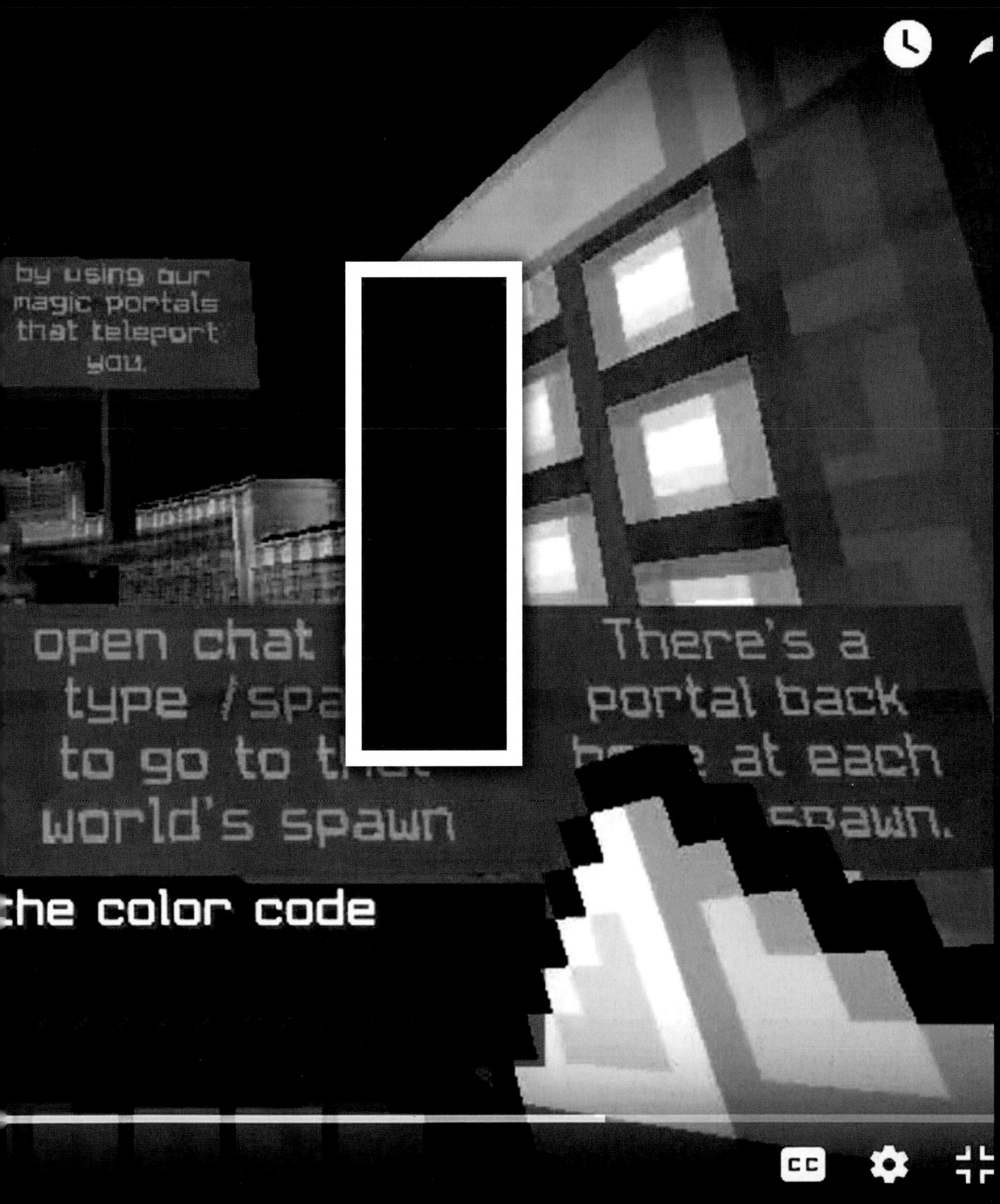

by using our magic portals that teleport you.

open chat
type /spa
to go to th
world's spawn

There's a
portal back
at each
spawn.

the color code

INACTIVITY:

Some hosts remove accounts of players who haven't visited the site in a while. They usually post this ahead of time on their server rules, so be sure to take note when you sign up. Some servers, like Cubeville, will let you post a leave of absence in their Vacation forum if you also leave a sign at your base that you'll be back soon.

INTERCRAFTEN:

Think of the coolest semi-grown-up in your life. It's probably a camp counselor. Intercraften was founded by a cool camp counselor who had such great success creating a server for his campers that he decided to take it online and open the world to a whitelisted group of players. The server has been around for years at this point and it seems to keep growing in popularity, so this is yet another example of a server you can be sure to find other people to play with no matter what your time zone is or what time you log in. There are challenges, mini-games, lots of worlds to check out, and a money system with jobs.

The server is heavily moderated with filters and griefing rollback protection to fix your build if you've been griefed. Apply to join the whitelist at www.intercraften.org. Visit www.intercraften.org/map for a live server map that gets updated every hour. Log in to server ID: 184.95.34.125:25565.

Visit the Intercraften website for a live map and other updated information about gameplay.

BLOGGER'S TIP: USE THE MENU BOOK!

"In addition to doing stuff with the usual server commands, such as /spawn, /sethome, and /home, you can consult the user-friendly Intercraften Menu Book (given free when you join) to help you pick jobs, perform commands, and play mini-games."

—Matt Doyle, Brightpips.com

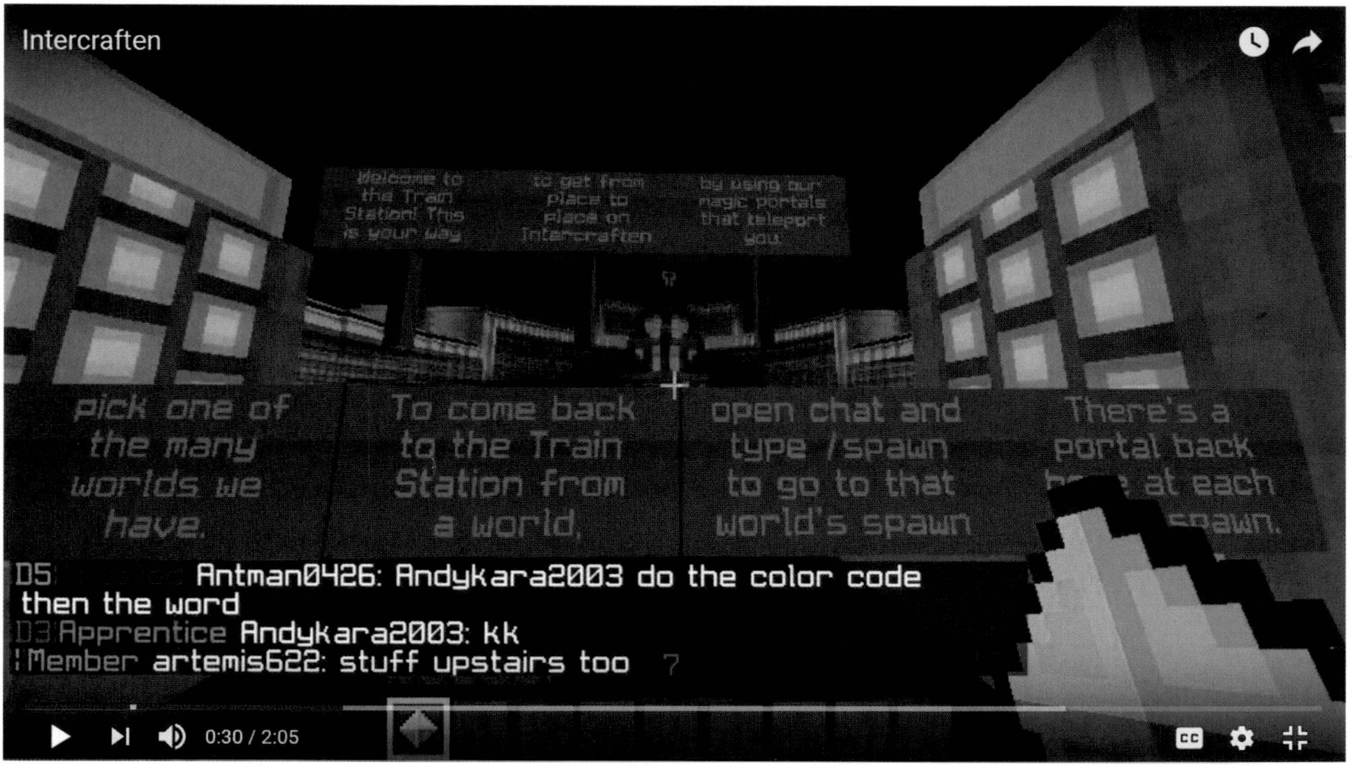

The Intercraften server lets you choose a job (like fisherman or woodcutter) and pays you in coins so you can purchase items at the store. The site features magic portals that will teleport you anywhere you want to go.

IRC, OR INTERNET RELAY CHAT:

There is a chat feature in Multiplayer mode that you can toggle on and off by typing the letter *T* while you're playing. But if you want to access chat outside of the server you're on to tell your friends where to meet up, get help with Minecraft from experienced users, consult a wiki of already answered questions, or just talk about stuff, you can download IRC chat software and visit official Minecraft-specific channels. There are rules that must be followed on each channel, of course. You need a parent's permission before downloading the software and you must remember to keep your personal information private and safe from strangers at all times when you're chatting.

Start with the two basic channels first:

- #Minecraft—This is the original channel made by the game's creator, Notch. It gets 500 to 600 users a day, and people talk about Minecraft stuff as well as just about anything at all, as long as it doesn't break any rules.

- #Minecrafthelp—This is the main support channel where you can ask for support, report possible bugs or problems, and get help.

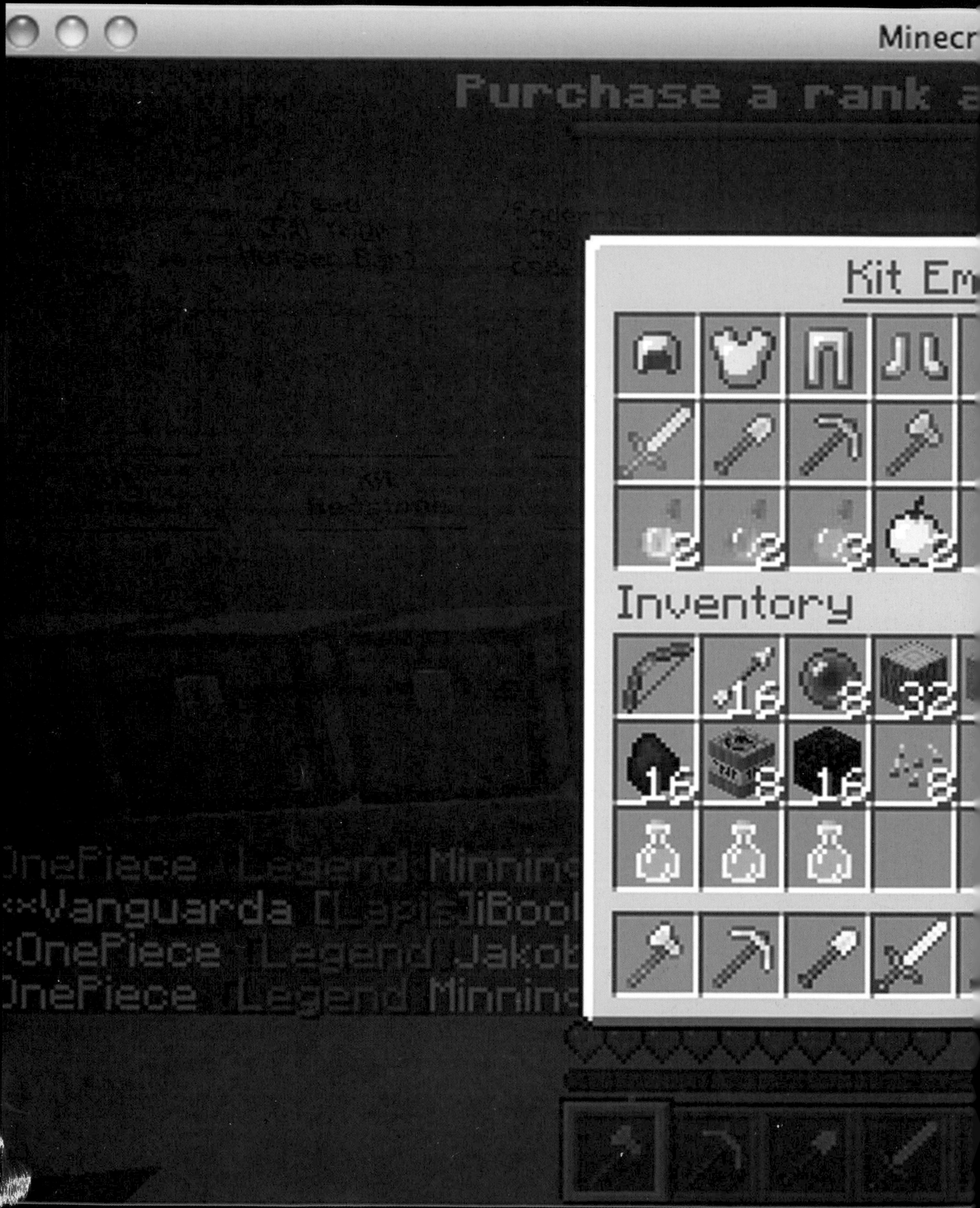

Minecr

Purchase a rank a

Kit Em

Inventory

OnePiece Legend Minning

<<Vanguarda [Lapis]Bool

<OnePiece Legend Jakob

OnePiece Legend Minning

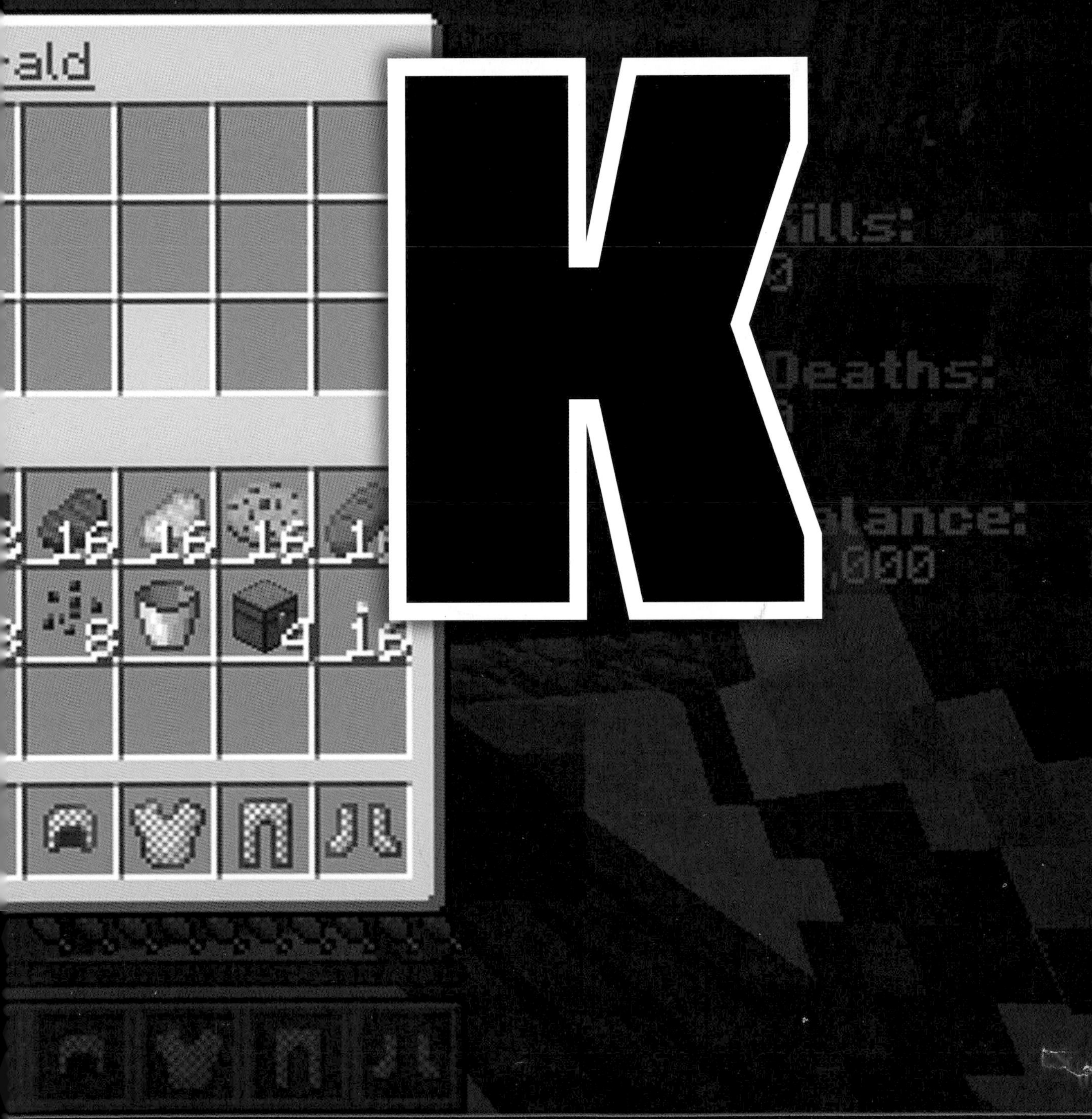

1.10.2
www.MCCentral.org
rald
K
ills:
Deaths:
alance:
,000

KITPVP:

In a Kit PvP game, you choose from a preset category of kits. Each kit is equipped with its own set of unique items. Enter battle with the kit of your choice to fight against your opponents to earn points, reputation, and achievements.

Hypixel is one server that offers Kit games. For example, in Skywars, each player or team spawns on their own island and the aim is to be the last player or team alive. Each time you kill a player, you are rewarded with a soul. You can use those souls to unlock kits and perks to improve your game experience.

Hypixel also offers UHC Kit PvP games where UHC stands for Ultra Hardcore mode. The only way to regain health is through golden apples and brewing potions in a fast-paced fight for survival.

This is an example of one kit you can choose from in a PvP factions game.

Wit

L

Death
ASFJerome
CraftBattle
TBNRfrags
Vikkstar12

LAG:

When your in-game character gets stuck in place or isn't responding in time with your input, you are experiencing lag. Overloaded servers can sometimes cause this delayed or stuttering effect during gameplay and it can be extremely frustrating to deal with. If the timing is bad, lag can cost you your player's life. WTFast, Optifine, and other downloads can help, but sometimes it's best just to find a less crowded server.

LAN:

A LAN, or a local area network, is a group of computers and devices linked to the Internet through the same server. Usually that's your home network, school, apartment building, neighborhood, office, or library. When you play a multiplayer game over a LAN, it's only available to other people on the same network.

To open your single-player world up to other players in your home network, open chat and type /publish or go into the Game Menu and click "Open to LAN." Select the game mode and other options, and you're good to go. Once you're all set, you'll get a message with an IP players can use to access your game. It wil say something like "Local game hosted on hostname:98765."

Your friends can now connect to your game using the link that popped up or, even easier, open the Multiplayer menu and scan for LAN Worlds. Every player must connect with a unique account—two players will not be able to connect using the same account or username.

PORT FORWARDING

When is a LAN not a LAN? When you set up port forwarding on your router. If you do that, then your friends and family can connect directly by typing in your IP and port. That will look something like this: 123.45.67.89:43787.

Always get an adult's permission before setting up port forwarding on your router or changing any settings on your home network outside of the game.

Selecting your settings to create a local area network game on your home network.

LAND PROTECTION:

See Claims.

LANDING ZONES:

Noobs usually have time to get acquainted with a new server when they are dropped into a landing zone. Here they'll encounter signs and instructions to get them started and, possibly, a tutorial to help them figure out whom to contact for questions or when they need to report griefers.

LOCK PROTECTION:

Lightweight Chest (LWC) and Residence are two types of single-block protection plugins that protect both the block itself and the contents of chests, furnaces, and dispensers. It can also protect any other blocks, and by default will protect doors, signs, and trapdoors. Some servers have LWC, Residence, or another locking system enabled to let you protect your home and inventory from griefing and theft.

Stow your valuables in a safe place before entering a survival arena.

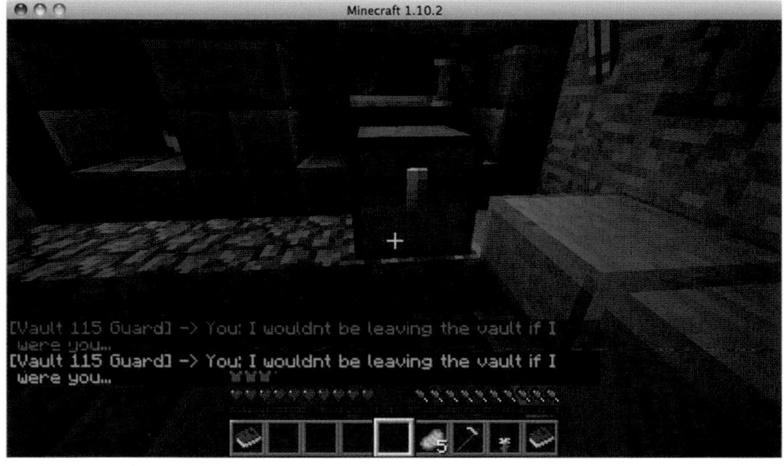

There are locked chests in prison worlds and other PvP servers where only certain players have access to the goodies inside.

LUCKY BLOCK:

Lucky Block is a mod that adds a new block to the game that can be placed and destroyed. When destroyed, it will not drop itself like most MC blocks. Instead, something happens at random—some valuable items drop, a trap spawns and kills the player, or a few dangerous mobs appear. The possibilities are endless and there are also lots of add-ons that create new types of Lucky Blocks.

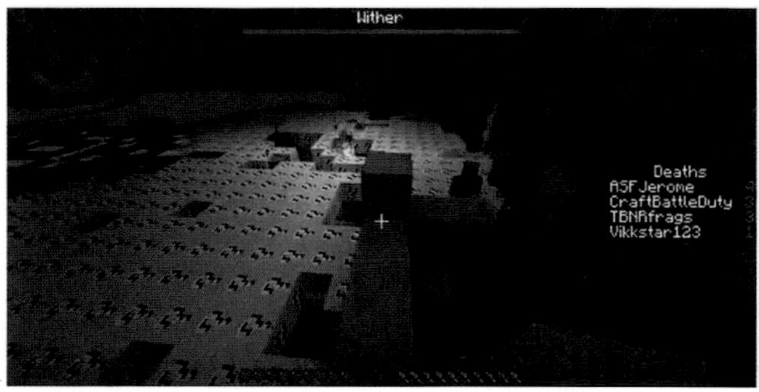

Try your luck at Lucky Block!

TheAceDuck has captured a Super Bacon and
blocks!

M
PARTY GAMES 1
www.hypixel.net

MCBALL:

A world dedicated entirely to paintball, MCBall offers free kits you can select before the game starts to give you special abilities or items you can use for an advantage over other players. Kits can include special guns, defenses, abilities—like Spider to let you climb walls and trap people in webs—and lots more.

Are you a whiz at making game maps? Do you have an idea for the ultimate paintball playing field? MCBall lets you submit your maps for consideration. If selected, your map can become an official playing field.

But what do I get if I win? you may ask. The game keeps track of the number of times your character dies and the number of kills you have and turns them into a ratio—a number that shows how your performance stacks up. You start with a bare head—no helmet—and earn a leather, iron, gold, diamond, or chain helmet depending on your score. If you win a tournament, you earn an enchanted helmet to show off your mad paintball skills.

MCBall games last 30 minutes, so if you have a half hour to spare, log on and try your skill!

A paintball game in MCBall.

Visit http://MCball.net to learn more. Log in to server ID: play.mcball.net.

MCMAGIC:

Disney World fans rejoice! Thousands of volunteer cast members and more than 500,000 guests have worked together to recreate the magic of the Walt Disney World resort in Orlando, Florida, on an MMO Minecraft server. The server offers a complete working theme park with rides, shows, and attractions. Here are some of the highlights.

Family-friendly thrill rides abound. At MCMagic Parks, you can explore four theme parks, two water parks, and multiple themed resorts filled with endless enchantment, where your fantasy becomes reality. Plus, you get to meet and play with new friends from all over the world!

Every ride that exists at the real Disney World in Florida is included for free, from immersive rides that contain actual audio, to fully working animatronics, to special effects. Each time you enjoy a ride you might find something different and cool to see, so keep your eyes and ears open. You never know what you might find.

It's just like being there in real life. You can revel in a street party, catch spectacular fireworks extravaganzas, and snap screenshots with your favorite characters. The fireworks happen every day, multiple times, so no matter what time you join you are sure to catch at least one show. And MCMagic characters can be found throughout the parks—meet them all and collect their signatures in the autograph book you'll find in your inventory.

Almost every day at the park there is a Festival of Fantasy Parade, which includes spectacular, state-of-the-art floats starring characters from some of your favorite Disney stories, plus colorfully costumed performers that actually move down Main Street, U.S.A. You can also enjoy live shows featuring many of your favorite characters, like Anna and Elsa's Sing-A-Long and the Indiana Jones's Stunt Spectacular at Hollywood Studios, or Stitch's Great Escape in the Magic Kingdom.

If you're curious or too excited to wait for your first real-world visit to Disney World, a virtual ride-through is a great way to experience the thrill from the comfort of your own computer so you'll know what to expect before you go! Visit https://palace.network to learn more. Log in to server ID: mcmagic.us.

A SECRET WONDERLAND FOR DISNEY FANS

- MCMagic has been around for more than five years. That's longer than most any other servers in the history of the game. Since 2011, over a million unique guests have enjoyed the parks.
- MCMagic Parks holds the record for the largest theme park server for three years in a row. They are featured in the 2015, 2016, and 2017 *Guinness Book of World Records* Gaming Editions.
- When you join, you get a MagicBand, an autograph book, and more—all for free.
- The shows and fireworks have both audio and text to make the play more accessible to all children.

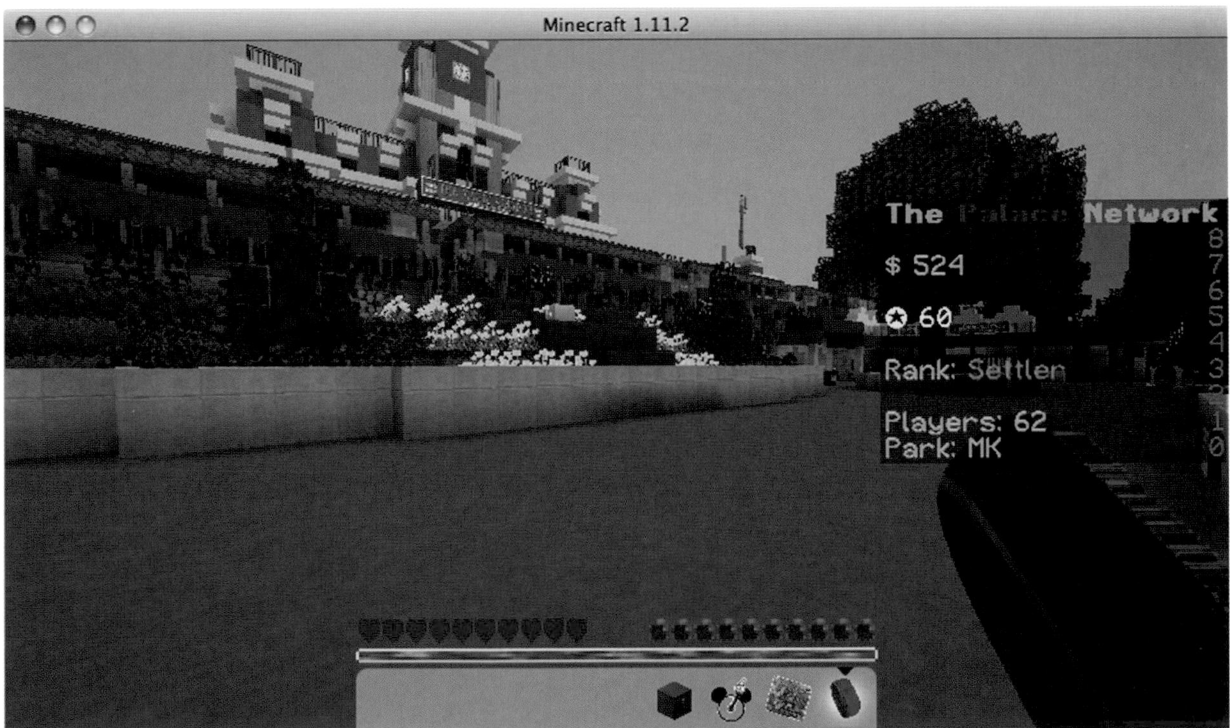

Take a virtual trip to Walt Disney World, the Happiest Place in Minecraft.

Since days only last 10 minutes, you don't have to wait long to experience the parks at night!

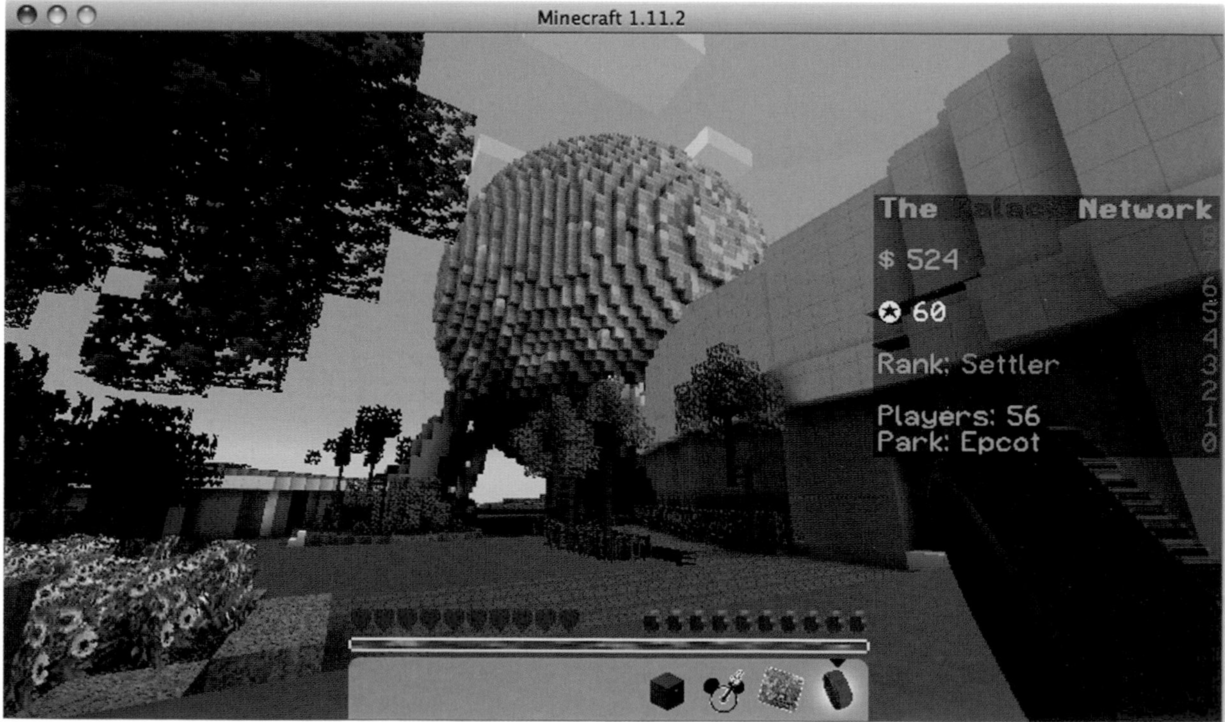

Epcot is one of the many famous landmarks you'll encounter in this virtual amusement park.

It gets pretty crowded at MCMagic, but you'll always have a good view!

MCMMO:

McMMO is a Bukkit plugin that turns a Vanilla world into an opportunity for playing games. McMMO expands the core game mechanics, adding role-playing game (RPG) modifications that feature unique skills to train and level in, and providing fun options to compete, level up, and rack up achievements. Many servers add the McMMO plugin to help them customize their servers for a unique experience.

MC SURREALCRAFT:

Fight on at Surrealcraft, a server focused on Factions and Kit PvP. Griefing—and more specifically, raiding—is actually allowed and encouraged. Admins will ban players for bad behavior on chat, however, and the server is whitelisted, which makes gameplay safe yet still fun for players who get into competition, factions, and playing tricks on each other.

Here's the unique part of MC Surrealcraft: the world itself is small. The creators felt that a more condensed world made the competition fiercer and more exciting, and lots of players agree!

Be warned that there is no chest protection, so you will need to rely on your own cleverness to protect your belongings and your base. The server runs McMMO, providing RPG-style level stats.

Visit http://mcsurrealcraft.com/home to learn more and to apply for the whitelist. Log in at server ID:Play.mcsurrealcraft.com.

Watch your step when wandering around the world of Surrealcraft. Lava pits aren't the only traps you may fall into if you're not careful!

MIDDLE EARTH:

If you've ever read *The Lord of the Rings* or *The Hobbit* or seen the movies, you know what an unusual and gigantic world author J.R.R. Tolkien created in his imagination. The folks at Minecraft Middle Earth had a goal back in 2010 to recreate the entire world he designed. They recruited volunteer builders to work with them, and the world has been expanding ever since. It is available and freely accessible for everyone. The site reports that since they opened they've had more than 12 million visitors, many of whom are active contributors!

Through the use of Minecraft, contributors create a virtual world with Minecraft blocks. Members create and design their own buildings, textures, landscape, sound and music, and more.

The creators note that they are only building the world, they are *not* a role-playing server nor are they hosting a videogame. The team works to design a fantasy world out of Minecraft blocks and provide a creative environment.

Middle Earth is a protected world, meaning you can't just build anywhere you want. Middle Earth designers have the ability to start jobs in which registered players can participate. During these jobs, the designer can make some areas buildable for everyone.

Occasionally, Middle Earth has Freebuilds or contests on Plot World within their Build server, but building outside of those contests and Freebuilds is prohibited.

A SECRET WORLD FOR *LORD OF THE RINGS* FANS

"Minecraft MiddleEarth creates the world by organizing projects and involving our members to show off their creativity. Major landmarks, terrain, houses, and decorations are man-made and our own original work. Players have access to Creative mode and a range of re-textured blocks to build in Gondor, Rohan, The Shire, Moria, or Mordor."
—Nicky Vermeersch, founder of Minecraft MiddleEarth

Middle earth staff photo in front of Minas Tirith, the newest big city build.

There are always people at work building in Minecraft Middle Earth.

Interior builders working hard in Minecraft Middle Earth.

The site uses TeamSpeak for designers and team leaders to communicate with their building teams, although many users often log in to chat with other Middle Earth contributors and have virtual hangouts. This long-term community has even trickled out into the real world, with an annual official "get-together" in Belgium during De Gentse Feesten, a folklore festival. People come to the festival from the United Kingdom, Germany, Sweden, Norway, and Poland to meet up at an official gathering.

Reminder: Play smart, stay safe: never meet anyone you've met online in person or give out personal information, including your last name, school, hometown, or names of anyone you know. If you want to go to an official meet-up, it must be confirmed and arranged by your parent or guardian. Report anyone asking for your personal information or to meet up in person to site moderators.

Visit www.mcmiddleearth.com to learn more. Servers can be found at:

Build Server: build.mcmiddleearth.com

PvP and Event Server: pvp.mcmiddleearth.com

TeamSpeak: ts.mcmiddleearth.com

MINEAGE FACTIONS:

One big world, lots of battles. If you like Factions, you'll love spanning the giant landscape of Player versus Player action with raiding, last-man-standing game mode, a random wilderness teleport system, and a super insane end PvP zone. While it's not a whitelisted server, there is always a staff member online to offer help or just say hello.

Blowing stuff up is part of the fun in Mineage.

MINEPLEX:

Mineplex is one of the largest, most popular Minecraft multiplayer servers. Enter the game through the lobby, which is a main sky island surrounded by a few smaller ones. You can do Parkour to earn gems, play stacker, and discover hidden secret rooms and Easter eggs in the lobby. From the lobby, you can access gaming areas and special events. The server offers four types of mini-games: classic, arcade, survival, and champions. Champion games lets players customize their character's stats and skills to compete against others. The server will also host special events on holidays like Halloween and Christmas, where players can earn event-exclusive prizes by completing the challenges. Players earn gems, which act as currency to buy items within the game. Visit http://mineplex.com to learn more. Log in to the server IP: mineplex.com.

LOVE KARAOKE?

Mineplex hosts karaoke parties where you can use **TeamSpeak** to sing in front of everyone at the party! Download and install TeamSpeak 3, set up your username, and log in to the Mineplex multiplayer server when it's time for the party.

Mineplex features a fast-paced mini-game called Bomb Lobbers, where players basically just throw TNT at each other and watch stuff explode.

MINESQUISH:

Sometimes you enter a world and it's so big, you feel like you could spend years trying to explore it all. That's Minesquish, a Vanilla Minecraft server that is as expansive as it is kid-friendly. It has so many unique worlds to explore and games to play that you will never be bored here.

Shinon, the main server, is composed of plots of land players can claim to build their own permanent home in the game. There is also a borderless exploration world. Players are also given their own storage locker called The Void where they can stash their loot securely and hide it from other players. There is also a Freebuild world and a competitive building world where contests are held.

That's the upside. The downside is that in a world this big, it can be challenging to find other players, and you may end up wandering around by yourself for a while looking for them. This server is whitelisted, so fill out the application for a quick approval, then spend some time looking around the world.

Stop to read the signs posted in each world. Not only are they full of information, but they're also pretty funny! If you like what you see, invite friends to apply as well, then make plans to meet up for some PvP exploration, building, play, and IRC chatting. Visit http://indiesquish.com to apply.

There is plenty of room to unleash your creativity in Minesquish. Here's one player's creative castle build.

Minesquish is a friendly place to visit!

MINI-GAMES:

Mini-games are small game modes in Minecraft, mainly on Minecraft servers. A mini-game can last from several minutes to a few hours and ends with a winner. One mini-game round has nearly no relation to any other mini-game round, so everyone starts with equal status. Good examples of mini-games are **Survival games** or **Spleef.** The largest Minecraft servers are basically mini-game networks, which means that they offer many different mini-games in many different rounds at the same time and provide an easy way to play different game modes with friends and other players.

In the Deathrun mini-game, there are two teams: Runners and Deaths. Runners must make it to the end of the map without getting killed. There are automatic death traps along the way that need to be avoided. The objective of the Deaths is to kill the Runners before they get to the end.

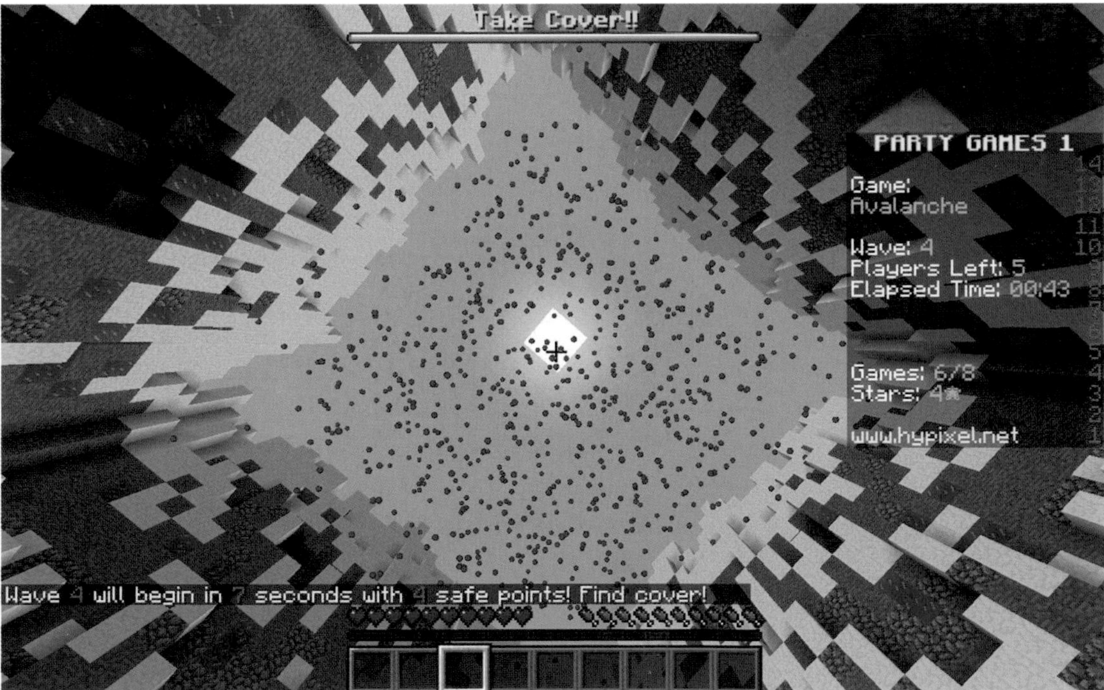

In this intense mini-game called Avalanche, players try to be the last one to survive a treacherous onslaught of falling snow.

Pig Fishing is a hilarious mini-game where you score points by trying to catch the most pigs on your fishing line. Turn up the volume when you play so you can hear every little grunt and squeal.

MMO (MASSIVELY MULTIPLAYER ONLINE):

An MMO is a game that can be played online and allows lots of people from anywhere in the world to meet up and play together. Minecraft is one of the most popular MMO games. It can also be called an MMORPG, which is an online role-playing game where people can take on an identity—like a Minecraft username or ID—with an avatar and maybe even a separate personality or backstory. Your Minecraft username stays with you wherever you go, and when you play online a lot, you may run into players you have faced in other sessions or even on other servers. If, like most players, you watch YouTube videos about Minecraft in your spare time when you're not actually playing the game, you'll start seeing names you recognize and start following YouTubers whose videos you like more than others. They usually put their usernames out there in the video. If you are lucky enough to run into one of these celebrities in a mini-game, say "Hi!" It's always nice to be recognized.

MOD, OR MODIFICATIONS:

Mod is the short form of modification and refers to small, programmed additions to the regular Minecraft game. One of the reasons Minecraft became so popular is that it offers the ability to customize the game as much as you like to make it your own, like adding new animals, inventing new items, or adding a minimap for better orientation. Officially, mods are not developed or supported by Mojang. All the work to make mods possible—a mod loader or a mod download database—is completely developed and distributed by the community.

Some modifications give players an unfair advantage and are considered hacks, including x-ray mods, x-ray texture packs, ore finders, Fly/Speed mods, and Inventory/Item mods. They may be banned from use, so check the server rules before using.

MODS, OR MODERATORS:

Moderators can be system administrators or players who help moderate chat rooms, answer questions on the boards, and assist new players.

Arthur_Lancelot gibbed DiaSchwert
RA1st gibbed skilegosnow
RA1st is on a Killing Spree!
Sneaking is disabled!
BabyLime gibbed mrcool6
Valkeos gibbed chr1smart1n
BabyLime gibbed skilegosnow
ts107gamers gibbed MrHelloMan
RA1st gibbed ts107gamers
Sneaking is disabled!

N

NAME TAG:

When you're in a multiplayer game, you'll see that every player's screen name (or name tag) hovers over his or her character at all times. Your name tag is visible to other players as well. Name tags make playing more fun because they allow you to send messages to specific players in chat. Color-coded name tags are also helpful as an instant indicator of who's on your team and who's not.

TIP

When playing multiplayer hide-and-seek games, or any game where being out of sight gives you an advantage, a name tag can get you seen and killed. Stand behind tall objects to hide your name tag and keep the advantage.

You can tell these three Quakecraft players are on the same team because their name tags are all blue.

NOOBSTOWN:

This server was one of the first Town servers in the Minecraft gaming community. It's a strictly managed, family-friendly server that includes anti-swear plugins and offers lots of worlds for hours of building and exploring. Your journey begins when you spawn in the garden of the Noobstown castle for your first tutorial. The registration process requires a little patience, but it's worth the wait.

Once you're a member of the Noobstown community you will be introduced to the server by Bernard the villager and you'll have three really cool districts to explore: the market district, where you can buy items that you need; the wizard district, a unique environment that hosts various special events; and the wilderness, where you will spend most of your time building a home and joining a town. Much of the town land is already settled by other players, but press on to the outskirts of the wilderness and you should still find an area to call your own.

There are five worlds in Noobstown, including the regular world where you wander through the wilderness and the mining world where you can mine the resources you need. You may also want to explore the events world to see what cool events are going on or to find portals to PvP challenges.

To explore the world yourself, log in at server IP: noobstown.com.

1

OMNIKRAFT:

Omnikraft is a player-focused community with a super-welcoming philosophy. The server welcomes members to the family and even promises to be there for you when you're having a bad day. Run by a small staff, the server has been around since 2013 and has thousands of dedicated members, so you're sure to have company to play, build, or battle with when you log in.

Their survival server features an innovative mod called a wilderness warp. It's a teleporting mechanism using command blocks to teleport a player randomly in the Overworld. It helps you find a good spot without having to walk for days to find the perfect spot to call your own.

The owners, Kryptix and MrPeppah, don't tolerate abusive, childish, and immature behavior, and they step in to help resolve any issues that may come up. The site offers weekly polls to get member input and they're always open to hearing new ideas and suggestions.

Visit https://omnikraft.net to learn more.

ADMINS FIGHT BULLIES

"I make it clear in our rules that we don't tolerate bullying and all staff encourage members to report anything that comes up. We try to talk through situations as much as possible with the players involved. Sometimes we mute them (where they can't talk in chat) or ban them for a period of time, generally to get those who are heated some time to cool down and think things through."
—Jimmy Tassin, Omnikraft founder

Players gathered at the dig arena in Omnikraft.

The Spawn City of Omnikraft.

The Omnikraft drop party in September, 2016.

OPTIFINE:

If you play around with a lot of servers online, even Vanilla or non-modded servers, you'll find that many of them use Optifine to help them run faster and look better. You may notice that servers that use Optifine have a smoother animation quality and more frames per second to make the movement more even. Then again, you may not notice it at all!

Mine

Reptaria » Sorry :C

P

PAINTBALL:

Run around in colored armor and shoot paintballs at your opponents! Paintball is a mini-game closest in gameplay to Capture the Flag, but players are equipped with several different types of paintball guns and colored armor, and are given a home base to store their equipment, reload, and retreat to. It's offered by many servers, including MCBall, which is a server dedicated entirely to paintball games, and Hypixel, which has many other games as well. Up to six teams can compete at a time.

PARKOUR:

Parkour in real life is a sport where people move quickly through an area by running, jumping, and climbing around obstacles. In Minecraft, there are servers dedicated to Parkour where maps are created for players to navigate by jumping; sprinting and jumping; leaping up, down, or diagonally; climbing ladders or walls; and jumping to bars or glass panes. The courses are fun, fast-paced, and difficult, though most servers have maps with different difficulty levels to help you train before you compete.

You can get different kits to boost your game play. To capture the enemy flag in Paintball, run up to it and bring it back to your own team's base without dying.

Parkour is difficult to master but fun to play.

Piratecraft is one of many servers that offer Parkour survival games.

PARTY:

Playing multiplayer online games is called "social gaming," and what better way to make gaming social than to host a gaming party? Several sites, including EvolveHQ, offer a free party system that gives players the ability to connect with friends online on a private party server and have video, voice, or text conversations with each other as you play. Sites will also help you discover other players to join up with for a game or mini-game that includes from two to an unlimited number of players. The difference between a gaming party and joining a regular server is that you can set up a private world for your group to play on with whatever restrictions or rules you want to set.

PAY TO PLAY:

It costs money to run a server, and server hosts need to pay for those costs. That's how pay to play became a part of the multiplayer experience. Most servers request donations to help cover their costs, and players who donate to the site are rewarded with bonus powers or

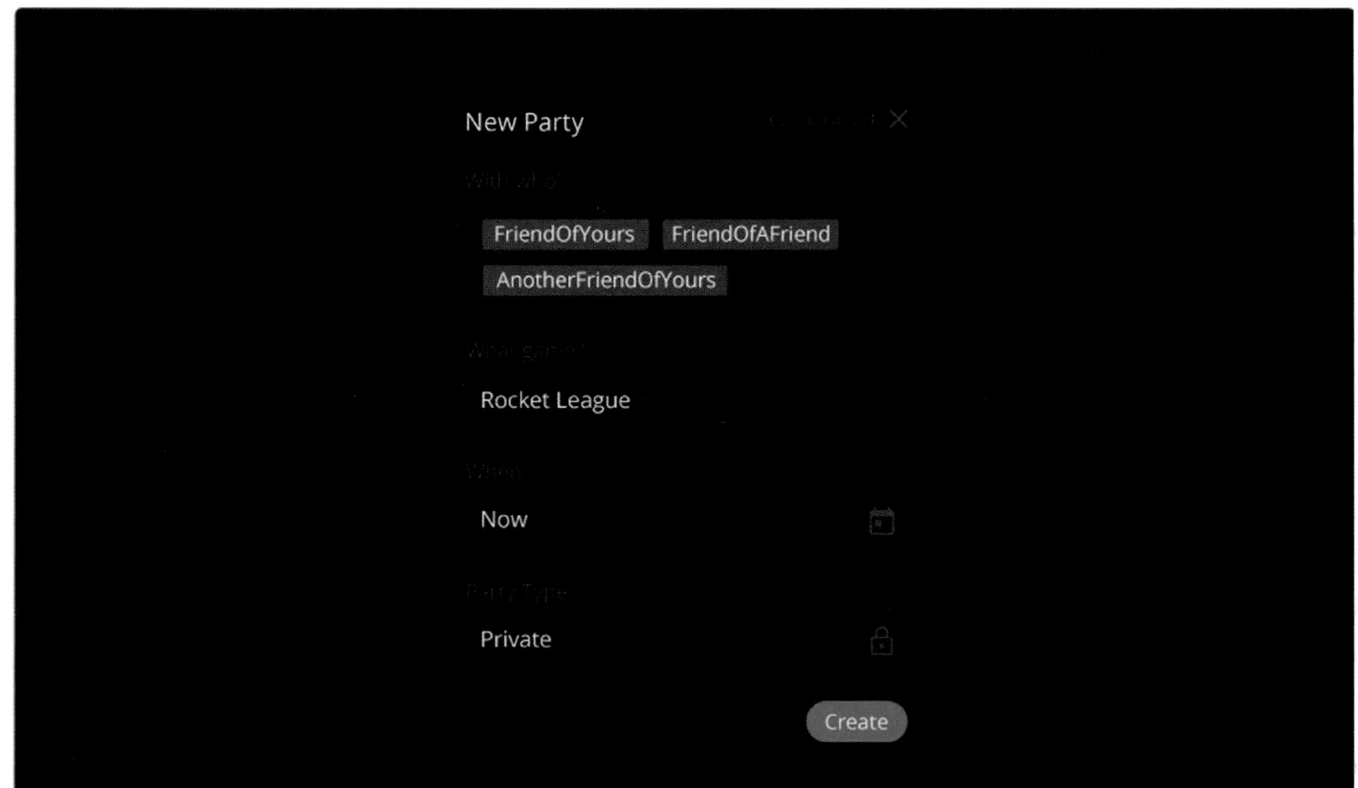

EvolveHQ lets you have a party with friends around the block or around the world.

points. There are other servers that take this further and offer premium status for players who pay a monthly fee. If you want to enjoy the site without paying, you may notice that you'll be excluded from privileges that others enjoy. For instance, you may have to wait longer in line for a popular game while premium members get to play first. Find servers that you like and that you feel comfortable using. For some users, pay-to-play is fine but for others it's annoying.

PING:

This is one of the stats you should use to evaluate a multiplayer server before joining. Servers with a low ping are better because they allow for faster updates of game data and help minimize the occurrence of lag. The lower the ping, the smoother your gameplaying experience. Internet connectivity issues and geographic distance can also contribute to high ping.

PIRATECRAFT:

Arrrr! Ahoy me, maties. If you're a fan of pirates or you just love the idea of sailing and plundering your way through a virtual world, a visit to PirateCraft is in order. Build a ship, equip it with cannons, and engage in ship-to-ship combat against other villainous thieves.

You'll be welcomed aboard the PirateCraft pirate ship.

There is a simple economy on land that allows for trade, and you can construct a house to create a safe zone where you can build as much as you like and stash your booty without fear of griefers or thieves. Be warned, though. When you're away from your ship, another pirate can steal it from you . . . but you can do the same. It's the law of the seas!

Visit piratemc.com to learn more. Log in at server IP: mc.piratemc.com.

PIXELMON:

If you've ever thought that combining two of your favorite things would make both even more awesome, you have to try Pixelmon. The Pixelmon modification is a fan-created mod that adds almost 300 Pokémon and about 500 fighting attack moves to the game to make it feel like a real Pokémon game. Even better, the mod comes with a Pokédex to keep track of your catches. In Multiplayer mode, you can even trade Pokémon with players you meet online.

Whether you want to play in Single-player mode or online through a server, you will need to download the mod at pixelmonmod.com. RC Pixelmon, Poke Gaming, RandomCraft, Destiny MC Pixelmon Network, PokeLegends, and Reach MC are some of the top Pixelmon whitelist servers you can join.

For a new way to experience Minecraft multiplayer games like Pixelmon, try pressing F5 to change your perspective from first person (where you are inside your character's body) to third person (where you are looking at your character from the outside).

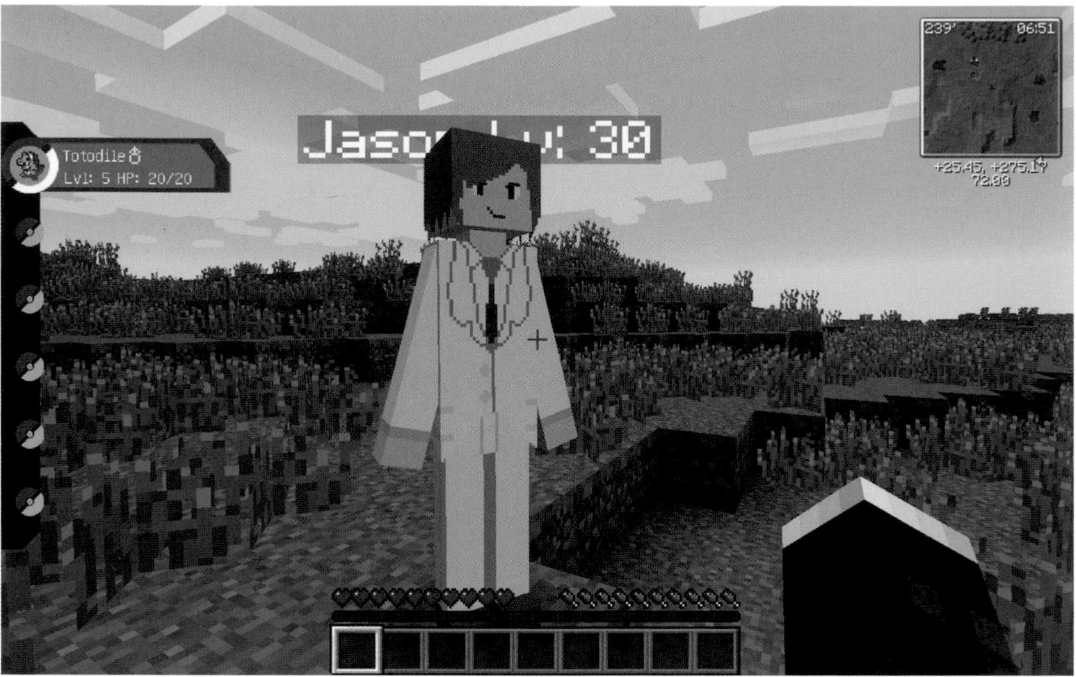

In Pixelmon, you'll find plenty of adorable Pokémon to capture and battle. When you encounter a trainer like this one, you can choose whether you want to battle.

You'll discover a lot of cool structures and Pokémon of all kinds while playing Pixelmon. The Pokédex in this player's hand will give her useful information about each Pokémon she encounters while exploring.

Aluminum ingot is a valuable resource in Pixelmon. You can use it to make all kinds of armor and weapons. You can also use aluminum ingots to make Pokéballs.

This Pokécenter is the perfect place to heal your Pokémon. You'll have an easier time finding one in the Plains Biome.

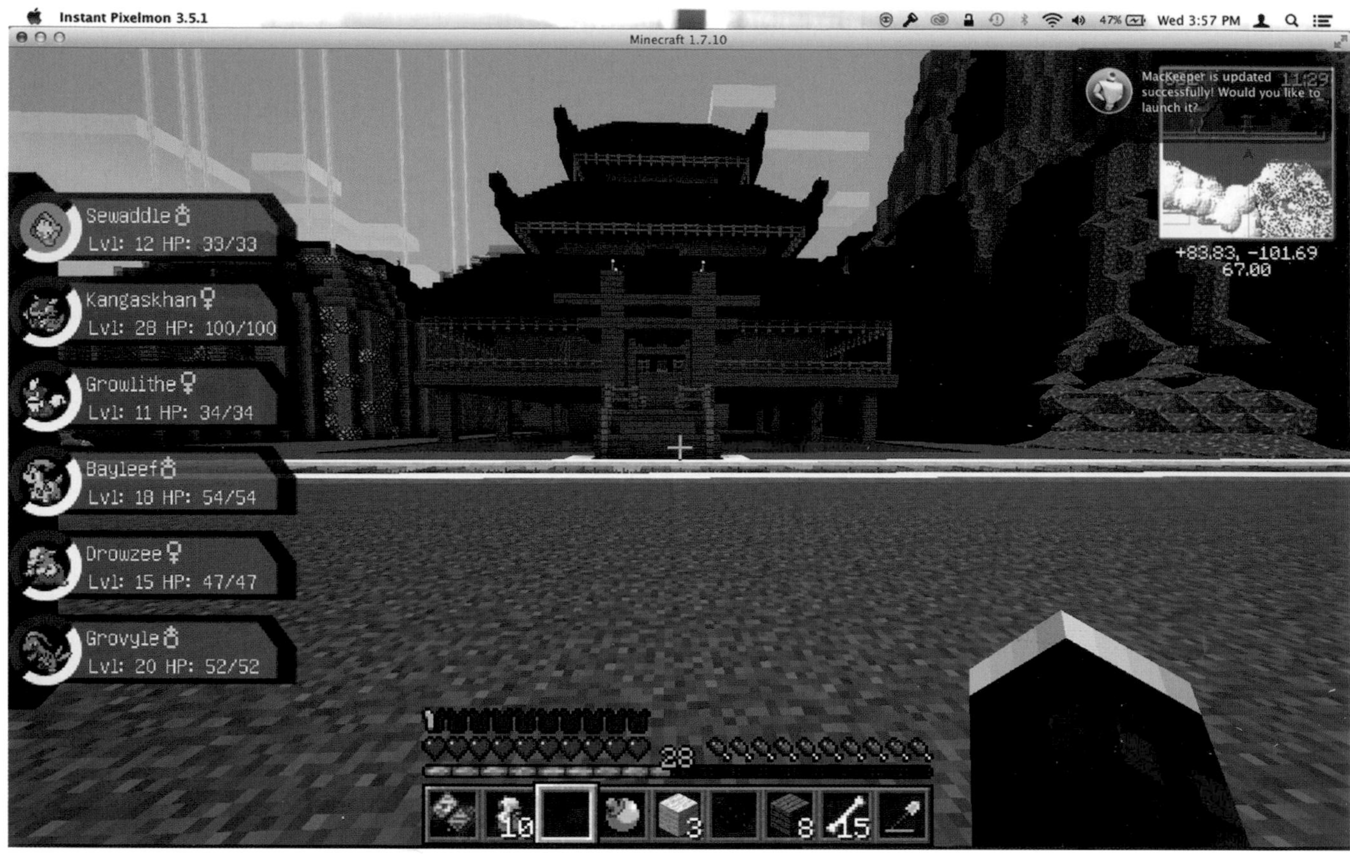

You might stumble upon a gym like this one while playing Pixelmon.

PixelmonCraft is a combo of two Pixelmon servers—one for the Kanto region and the other for the Johto region. Just like the Single-player mode mod, animals in the game are replaced with Pokémon, and can be caught and battled with. Fight gym leaders, shop at Pokémarts, and avoid the long-grass at all costs!

Log in to server ID: us.pixelmoncraft.net.

PLANETMINECRAFT:

PlanetMinecraft.com is the headquarters of all things Minecraft. It is an online community where players can share their creations, ideas, and games. You can learn about mods for your own server, find new ways to play, and find new servers to join in their easily searchable list. You can download shared projects, texture packs, skins, and mods to use on your own single-player home computer or in Multiplayer mode.

If you're passionate about Minecraft, this is a great community to join. There are many contests to enter, like skin design, world creation, blog posts, and charity events. Members come up with pretty mind-blowing designs and ideas. Browse entries and winners to get inspired to create your own. Visit the Community page to see if any players are live streaming their gameplay when you visit.

Visit Planet Minecraft online at planetminecraft.com and check out their projects, skins, and packs available for download. The Most Popular tab is the best place to start on your first visit.

You can upload your own creations, download amazing environments, or vote for your favorites while interacting with other Minecraft fans at Planet Minecraft.

PLUGINS:

Most servers extend Minecraft using server plugins, which allow for a whole range of extra gameplay features, including money systems, jobs, role-playing elements, and teleports. You can get plugins if you're running your own LAN game or server. If you join a server that already has plugins, you don't need to modify your Minecraft game to add these features; they're all handled by the server.

WHAT'S THE DIFFERENCE BETWEEN PLUGINS AND MODS?

Mods are modified code for playing Minecraft. They give you additional commands, change the game features, and work as the foundation for plugins. Mods need to be updated to keep up with Minecraft updates. CraftBukkit is one example of a mod. Plugins offer bonus features and don't usually require updating. Stargates and WorldGuard are examples of plugins.

POPULATION:

When you're using a survival server, population, or the number of players in the game at one time, can seriously alter your game experience. Anarchy-style servers are often more exciting when played with a lower population. More space to move around the world without bumping into other players means you have the room to find resources and ensure your own survival. It also adds to the intensity. For mini-games, a higher population of players is often a good thing. It means you can dive into a game without having to wait around for enough people to play.

PORTAL:

Gamers love portals because they serve as an instant shortcut to new and exciting worlds. In multiplayer mode, a portal can land you right in the middle of a new, unfamiliar challenge.

Dive right into this portal in the Hypixel lobby and you'll be teleported into some really exciting multiplayer games.

POTTERWORLD:

Fans of Harry Potter rejoice. You can play online, attend classes, brew potions, search for hidden chests, fight duels, learn spells, meet other students, and much more. This role-playing game has currency, a daily challenge, and a set of strict rules. The worst rule violations will get you insta-azkabanned!

Hogwarts recreated in Minecraft brick by brick is an impressive sight. Visit http://www.potterworldmc.com/ to find more amazing Harry Potter–themed Minecraft worlds.

Visit the site of some of your favorite scenes in the Harry Potter books and movies.

Once you join the server and get sorted into your proper house, your role-playing adventure kicks into high gear as you become a student at Hogwarts School of Witchcraft and Wizardry! Each player is equipped with a wand and can take live classes to learn spells.

Adult staff members are always online and available to help or step in to problem-solve. Potterworld is proud to be a family-friendly server.

PRISON:

Prison servers are servers without any wilderness. To progress on the server, players have to earn money in various ways, such as by farming resources in the prison to reach a higher level. The higher the level, the more areas that can be accessed. Some servers also have PvP enabled, so players can kill each other. PvE prison servers allow you to team up with other players or fight your way out solo to escape the prison. Prison Tech is an example of a prison server where the world acts as a prison.

It's split into several cellblocks, and the players role-play as prisoners attempting to break free. Senior players act as guards and wardens. In Prison Tech, players are forced to work in the mines and can sell stacks of mined elements to work their way up in the game. Beware as you reach higher levels, as play becomes PvP and you need to watch your back for more than just the prison guards. Log in to server IP: play.ge3knation.com.

PROP HUNT:

Prop Hunt is a PvP Hide and Seek or Block Hunt game where you become one of the twenty-six Minecraft mobs and work to find all your opponents before they find you. The winner is the player who finds the most opponents and manages not to get caught.

PVE:

PvE means player versus environment. In PvE, you're battling mobs and the elements to survive. In Multiplayer mode, you can team up with other players to support each other, form a community, and learn from each other's experiences. PvE servers can create mazes, mob spawners, custom maps, and challenges for players to overcome separately or as a team, with different goals depending on the task. You can rack up kills, loot, coins, XP (experience points), or other types of points to improve your score and compete against yourself or your opponents. Prison escape, dungeon, adventure maps, battle arenas, and monster spawners are a few examples of PvE servers.

PVP:

PvP stands for player versus player, and in these servers players compete for survival. In other words, players can kill each other and steal each other's gear. You'll usually find PvP on Survival and Vanilla (non-modded) servers. The theme here is hunt or be hunted . . . or both! And you have to be up for the challenge.

TIP

On a PvP server, arm yourself well before leaving your house and make use of locks on doors and chests if they're available. Stock up on potions and enchantments, wear armor, and carry a shield for protection. Retreat if your armor or weapons are running low, and stock up on milk and potions for healing. Sharpen your attack skills against hostile mobs in Single-player Survival mode, and figure out which weapons and strategies work best for you. Some people are sharpshooters with ranged weapons (bow and arrow), while others are better at melee attacks with a sword or an axe.

Many PvP servers, like those on Omnikraft, have set aside special arenas for full PvP action. When you enter a competition arena, you'll get a clear warning that you're about to enter a zone where you may be attacked by another player, and you'll have the opportunity to turn back if you want.

In this PvP mini-game called Infection Arena, one player is infected and tries to infect the other players in the arena before the timer runs out.

A warning message on MC Central to watch your back when entering a PvP zone.

Q

QUEST:

A quest, also known as QM or Questing mode, invites players to complete quests to gain rewards. The rewards might be cool items, loot bags, extra lives, or achievements.

HQM, or Hardcore Questing mode, gives you a limited number of lives—usually only one!—to complete your quest before your progress gets deleted.

There are lots of kid-friendly worlds to explore and quests to complete in Blocklandia.

G| [A Quick Dip] ~IllegalMoch >> Everythi
G| [A Quick Dip] ~IllegalMoch >> Claimed
G| [CoOwner] ~RedneckMama >> yeah...?
putting my ribbons

R

RANCH N CRAFT:

In Minecraft, there's truly something for everyone, as evidenced by the Western feel of Ranch N Craft's country environment. Saddle up and join this friendly, moderated server with a small-town feel. Claim land to start your own ranch, breed horses, and farm crops without fear of griefers or bad guys shooting up your homestead. If you're up for some peace and quiet and a friendly neighborhood, come on over and stay for a spell.

Visit http://ranchncraft.com for more information. Log in at server IP: mc.ranchncraft.com.

Ranch N Craft features a full working economy.

REALMS:

You can set up your own private server for you and your friends on Minecraft Realms, a paid server hosting service provided by Mojang, the creators of the game. You can invite as many friends as you like to play whenever they want, even when you're not online, but you can only host up to ten players at once.

Visit Minecraft's Realms page to set up your subscription—you can get a free trial if it's your first time signing up.

To play:

Open Minecraft and click Play.

Click on the Realms tab.

Click New Realm.

Name the Realm and select the duration and number of players.

Click Create and enter your Realm.

Open the main window to set gameplay mode to Survival or Creative.

Find friends and add them by clicking Add Players and typing in their Minecraft username.

That's it!

Create a realm of your own for a great place to meet up.

In Minecraft Pocket Edition, a player is welcomed into Realms.

RPG:

RPG, or role-play multiplayer servers, are Minecraft servers that provide an environment for its players to take on a personality and act as if their character is really that person. You may also hear it called MMORPG, which is just shorthand for calling it a massively multiplayer online role-playing game. One of the most common settings for a role-play server is the medieval era. It also fits best with the mechanics and items of Minecraft. The ways in which the role-play is implemented and enforced can differ a lot.

You can join an RPG server and take on the identity of a player in that world, whether it's a Pokémon character, a Hogwarts student, the owner of a McDonald's restaurant, a medieval villager, or anything the world creators can imagine. RPGs often have a skill leveling progression mod, custom maps with prebuilt terrain or buildings, plot manager mods, and other common server modifications like Griefing Protection and Inventory Protection to make gameplay more fun and exciting and to make their server unique.

Minecr
Latest Update

S

THE SANDLOT:

The Sandlot has been around since 2011, offering several game modes including a Normal-Difficulty Survival world, an Easy Difficulty world with jobs and a mall, a Creative world, a **PvP** server with arenas and **survival games, SkyBlock,** and **Parkour maps**.

Run by a parent who used to be a teacher, the Sandlot is pretty strict about swearing, being mean, and playing fair at all times. They enforce safety with a team of moderators who patrol the site all the time, as well as a strict chat filter, and a **whitelisted** server you need to be approved for by running your username through banned server lists and making sure applicants are who they say they are.

Visit the Sandlot at www.sandlotminecraft.com to learn more and apply for the whitelist. The server IP is: server.sandlotminecraft.com.

SEMI-VANILLA:

Semi-Vanilla is a version of multiplayer Minecraft servers that's restricted to a very limited use of plugins to offer an experience like **Vanilla,** but with a better protection and some helpful features. These servers are using **Spigot** or **Bukkit** as server software. Allowed features are basic teleports, to **teleport** to the spawn or to a set home point.

A very important reason to use Semi-Vanilla instead of Vanilla for a public server is to prevent **griefing** with protection and logging plugins. Also allowed are plugins that don't directly affect gameplay like chat or voting.

SERVERS:

Multiplayer games need a host server that runs the game and lets everyone connect to the game and to each other online or via a local area network (LAN). A server can be hosted in your house on your home computer or on a friend's computer, or it can be hosted by a business. The server host decides which mode the game runs on—Survival, Adventure, Creative, or Hardcore—and is in charge of everything—setting up games, creating worlds, making rules, and adding mods.

Servers are not the same as worlds. In fact, many servers host multiple worlds to play in and teleport between. When you begin your server experience, you enter these worlds through a central lobby.

Just like in the regular single-player game, there are different kinds of servers:

- Creative servers allow you to jump into a plot-focused world to develop whatever you want to build.

This is an example of what you'll see when you add a new server. Give the server a name—the name of the actual server if it's public, or a unique way to identify it if it's private—then type in the server ID. Double-check the address, especially if it's just a bunch of numbers. You won't get in if even one number or letter is incorrect.

- Mini-game servers let you build, play, and compete in mini-games.
- Modded servers have custom modpacks that offer extras like machines, magic, and automation.
- PvP servers allow you to team up or go solo to test your battle skills against other players.

If your server is outdated, you might see this message.

HOST YOUR OWN SERVER

Are you ready to take charge of your own world and play by your own rules? It's possible to set up a server just the way you like it and invite your friends.Trying to make this happen completely on your own would be very difficult. Fortunately, there are mods, packs, and online servers (like Aternos) that have done all the hard work for you so you're free to customize your social gaming experience more easily.

Server lists

Servers come and go, and some go on- and offline all the time. The best way to discover new servers is to check with friends so you can join them online, but if you're looking to find a new online experience, visit server lists like

Minecraft Server List and Minecraft Forum. Once you discover your favorite server, vote for it on the list to keep it going strong. A server is only as strong as the number of players who join it, so don't keep your favorites a secret.

You can search a server list by the type of gameplay you're interested in, such as Parkour or Hunger Games, or by the type of server, like whitelist.

Server lists will give you an updated list of which servers are online by displaying a banner. The banner can tell you how many people are currently playing so you can decide where to go before you log on, though the number isn't always correct.

EXPERT TIPS ON CHOOSING A SERVER

Many players rely on server lists to decide which server they are going to join. New players especially use search engines to find their first server, and the higher rated a server is, the more likely it will be at the top of the results.

Server lists provide basic information about a server, including:

- The uptime of the server and how long it has been around
- The rank of the server with the listing service
- The type of server it is and what it offers
- Other server information, such as version and description

The rank of a server is calculated based on the number of votes that a server gets, and this is where you come in. By voting for your favorite server on a number of server lists, you can help promote the server, improve its rank, increase its relevance, and get more people to join.

By voting, not only are you helping out your favorite site, but sometimes you can also earn in-game items, awards, or XP. Visit your favorite server's website to find out what you can earn by voting for your favorite server. You can vote every day!

—Jimmy Tassin, OmniKraft founder

SKINS:

Skins are a creative way to change your appearance in the game. If you want to stand out in a multiplayer setting, customizing your look is an easy way to do it. To change yourself from the default character and get a new exterior, go to Minecraftskins.net, PlanetMinecraft.com, or any other site with free skin downloads. You can choose from hundreds of creative options online, including your favorite television and movie characters. Imagine how much fun you'll have battling opponents dressed as Minnie Mouse or an Angry Bird! For the more artistic gamer, there are also programs for designing your own Minecraft skins.

SKYBLOCK:

SkyBlock spawns players on an "island" floating in the sky, creating a PvE—Player versus Environment—experience. Players must use the resources they are given to survive in the game, complete challenges, and earn rewards to help improve their island.

SkyBlock is a game that takes place in a land of floating islands.

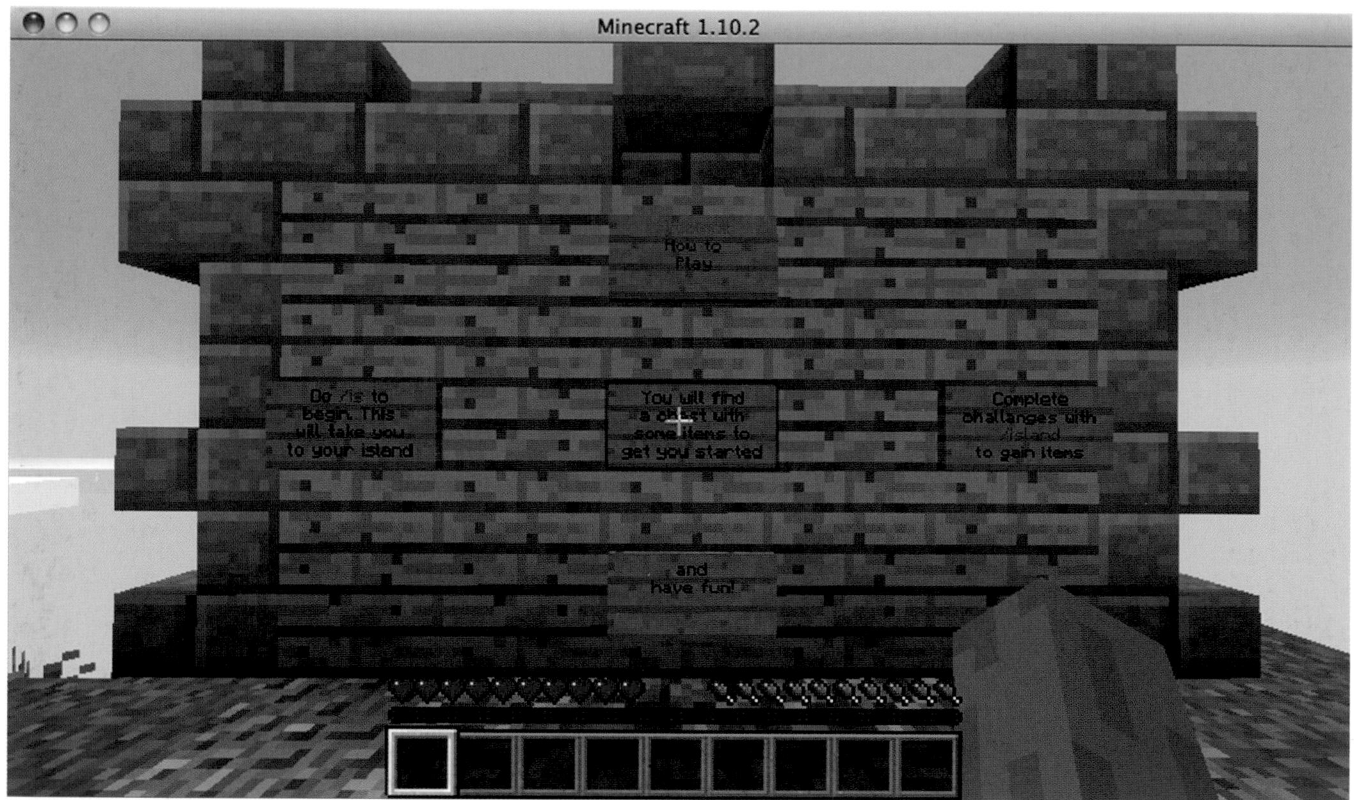

Some servers post game instructions on signs. Be sure to read the signs before playing.

SMODS:

SMods are moderators with a few more responsibilities. SMods have the ability to ban players and use "/god" to assist players.

SOCIAL GAMING:

Social gaming is about playing games and sharing that experience with others. Sometimes that experience is shared directly in a multiplayer experience; other times it is shared by sending friends updates, videos, screen captures, and streams of your latest gaming adventures. **EvolveHQ** is an example of a social gaming platform.

Part of what makes social gaming fun is that you get to meet new people who share the same interests as you. But just like any other form of social media, you should always be mindful of respecting yourself and others. Safety is always the number one priority!

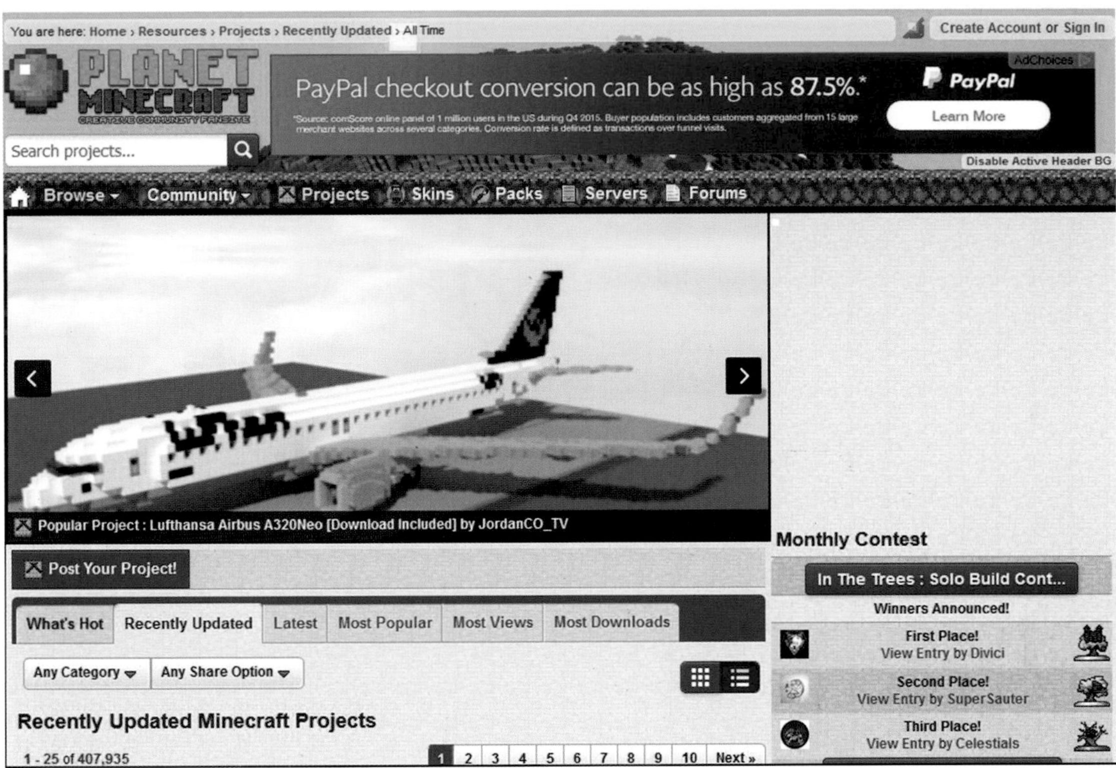

Planet Minecraft offers players an opportunity to share what they create and inspire others.

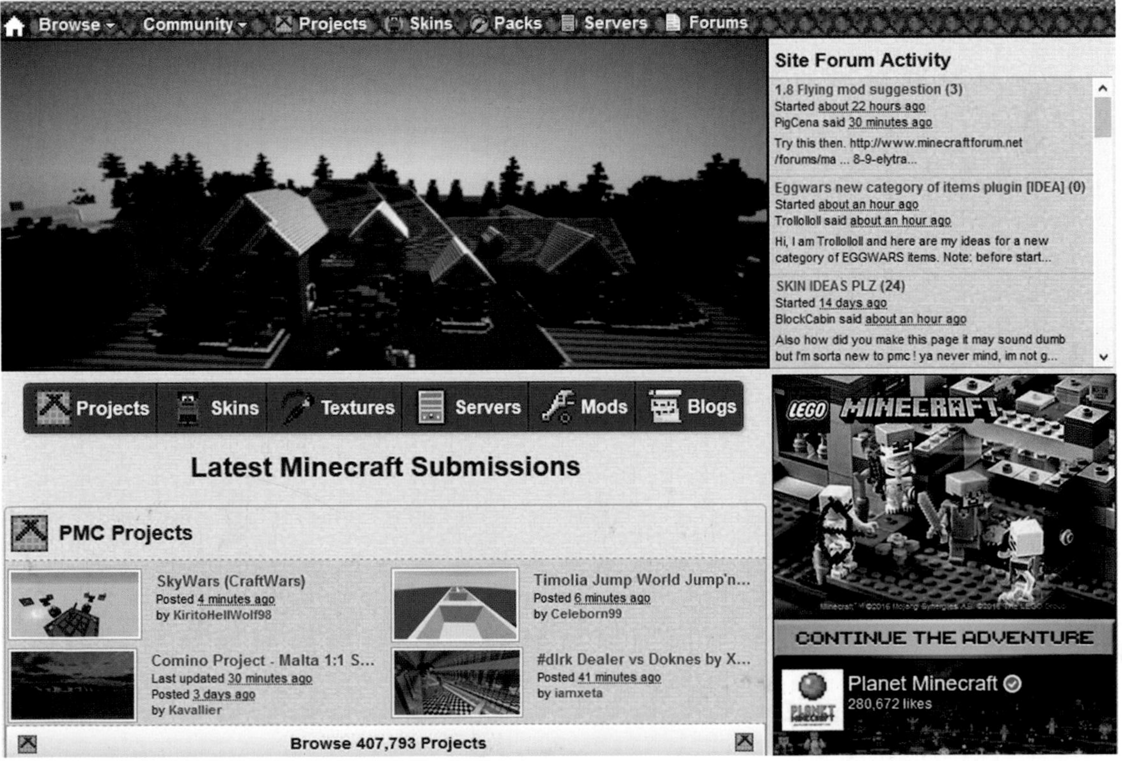

Submit your best creations on sites like Planet Minecraft.

SPAWN:

When you enter a world, you spawn (or begin) there in a set position. This spawn point is the point where you will start over again when you die in the game. You cannot modify anything in the immediate area around your spawn point (unless you are a server operator). If you need to go back to where you spawned, type the command /spawn and that should do the trick.

SPIGOT:

Spigot started as a Bukkit modification with the goal of improving the performance of Minecraft servers. After the end of the Bukkit project in 2014 Spigot took over the development of Bukkit itself and succeeded it. Today Spigot is the most common server software to be used with plugins.

SPLEEF:

Spleef rhymes with *grief* and that's basically what this mini-game is all about. To play, use a shovel to destroy blocks below other players to get them to fall off the playing field into a pit. The field is made of an easily destroyed block like snow, leaves, dirt, or clay. Gameplay is most similar to the classic board game Don't Break the Ice.

Spleef games on different servers may not look the same, but the gameplay is similar. Find your favorite server.

In the Hive, Spleef is called Splegg.

SURVIVAL SERVER:

A survival multiplayer server, or SMP as it's often called, is a Survival mode server that allows **PvP**, or Player versus Player, activity. While **griefing** is frowned upon on every good **whitelist** server out there, **hacking** (playing tricks on other players, setting traps, and engaging in some harmless trickery and tomfoolery) is allowed on Survival servers. Every server has its own rules and you should read and understand them before you sign on to play. SMP servers are designed to get players to collaborate, working together to build towns and cities, fight mobs, create communities, farms, and even build a working economy, depending on the server.

SURVIVAL GAMES:

The multiplayer mini-game Survival Games was adapted from the book and movie series, *The Hunger Games*. The players start with an empty inventory in a circle in the middle of a big arena: this can be a small town, a dark forest, or any other kind of Minecraft map. Crates filled with loot like weapons, armor, and food are spread everywhere on the map, especially in the middle. The players grab the loot from the crates to equip themselves and try to survive and kill the other players. Players who are "killed" are out of the game. The last one standing wins.

Hunger Games, shown here, is a popular survival game.

Could you survive the night if you spawned on a survival island like this one?

When you arrive in a new land, read the signs to discover your next challenge and learn the laws.

TNT
64
64
15
64

T

TEAMSPEAK:

TeamSpeak is a third-party application players use to talk using microphones and text chat. You must download and install TeamSpeak in order to access some collaborative servers, such as Middle Earth. To download it, visit the site that uses it and follow the instructions when you log in. For Minecraft Middle Earth, for example, visit www.mcmiddleearth.com/resourccs/tcamspcak-guide.44 to learn all about how to download, install, and use the software. Mineplex is another server that uses TeamSpeak. You can chat as you play or join events like karaoke parties to add your voice to the fun of online play.

TEXT CHAT:

Minecraft has built-in text chat (the *T* key), which is the default way to communicate with other players. Chat can be public or private. Most servers have automatic filters that won't let you swear in text chat, although many people find a way around it using spaces, punctuation, and misspellings to use inappropriate language. Some servers have other filters that turn off chat completely, restrict chat to only speaking with **admins** and **mods**, or limit chat to only those on a trusted friends list.

Remember: Never give out personal details when chatting.

TNTRUN:

TNTRun is a mini-game map that can be found on many multiplayer servers. Players start on a layer of sand. Since sand breaks apart every time you step on it, every block you step on disappears instantly. If you fall through the

The arena is filled with TNT and gravel blocks that fall when you step on them. Run through and survive for as long as you can!

Earn double-jumps to stay one jump ahead of disaster!

hole, you are knocked out of the game. The last player left is the winner.

TOWNCRAFT:

Towncraft is not whitelisted, so anyone can join—just enter play.towncraft.us into your Minecraft client. It also has a TeamSpeak server for voice chat; you can find the IP address on the Towncraft website. Although a non-whitelisted server with voice chat is usually a cause for concern, it's not that busy and there are parents and kids playing on the server when it does get crowded. People are generally friendly and helpful. Towncraft uses the Grief Prevention plugin so you can protect your house and contents from griefing by other players.

What is neat about Towncraft is that, rather than just being a standard world to explore and build in, it has a bit of a narrative going on. A meteor has wiped out the world, and it's up to you and your friends on the server to rebuild it. At the start of the game, you pick a trade, such as hunter, farmer, blacksmith, or merchant, and then as you improve your skills in that trade over time, you unlock new abilities.

The server uses the Zombie Apocalypse plugin; this randomly makes a horde of zombies appear around the player at night, which you must defeat to receive a reward. Obviously, younger players might get a bit freaked out by this, but it's good fun for older kids.

TIP

Don't hesitate to read the guide that the site admin put together for newbies and anyone else who wants to know more.

Most Towncraft visitors play in survival mode.

TOWNY:

Towny is a multiplayer server plugin that allows you to create a town in Minecraft, complete with a mayor, a bank, residents, and weekly taxes that residents pay. Players are allowed a certain number of town blocks to make a town, with a specific number of players allowed in each town depending on its size. An original town is made of 21 by 21 town blocks. As more players join a town, the town is given more blocks, allowing it to expand. Players work together to build and make their town flourish. Towns are protected from griefers and hostile mobs. A player is allowed to be part of one town at a time. Use the command /towny prices to view prices for creating a town. Use the command /town add <playername> to include specific players in your town. When towns join together, they create a nation, which allows for more land and lets residents participate in war events with other nations.

TROLLING:

Trolling is griefing with the intention of being really annoying. It's a subset of griefing and specifically refers to actions that are basically bullying. Some examples are killing people, destroying their items while they watch helplessly, promising to give people things and not handing them over, or giving people things and then killing them to get those items back.

While moderators can't block players from being trolls, a good moderator will warn or ban a reported troll. If you want to completely avoid being trolled, griefed, or bullied, play only on closed servers, on servers with Land Protection, or over a home network (LAN) with friends. Not sure if a behavior is trolling or just joking? If everyone thinks it's funny, it's a joke. If someone is annoyed because he or she has been harmed or inconvenienced, it's trolling.

Want to avoid being banned for trolling? Follow one simple rule: be nice!

TROUBLESHOOTING:

Unable to join a server? There are two main reasons you may not be able to connect.

If it's a private or whitelisted server, you need to get permission from the server administrators before you can log in.

If you've been granted access but still can't play, check to make sure you are using the same version of the game as the server, whether it's over a LAN or hosted on an outside server. Check the server FAQ to see which version of Minecraft it's running on. If they don't match, don't panic! It's easy to roll back your version to match the server you're playing on.

To change the game version, select New Profile from the game launcher, then select the game version that matches the server. You can set up different versions for different servers and switch between them depending on the server you want to use. The "Use version" dropdown in the topmost window lets you choose the version.

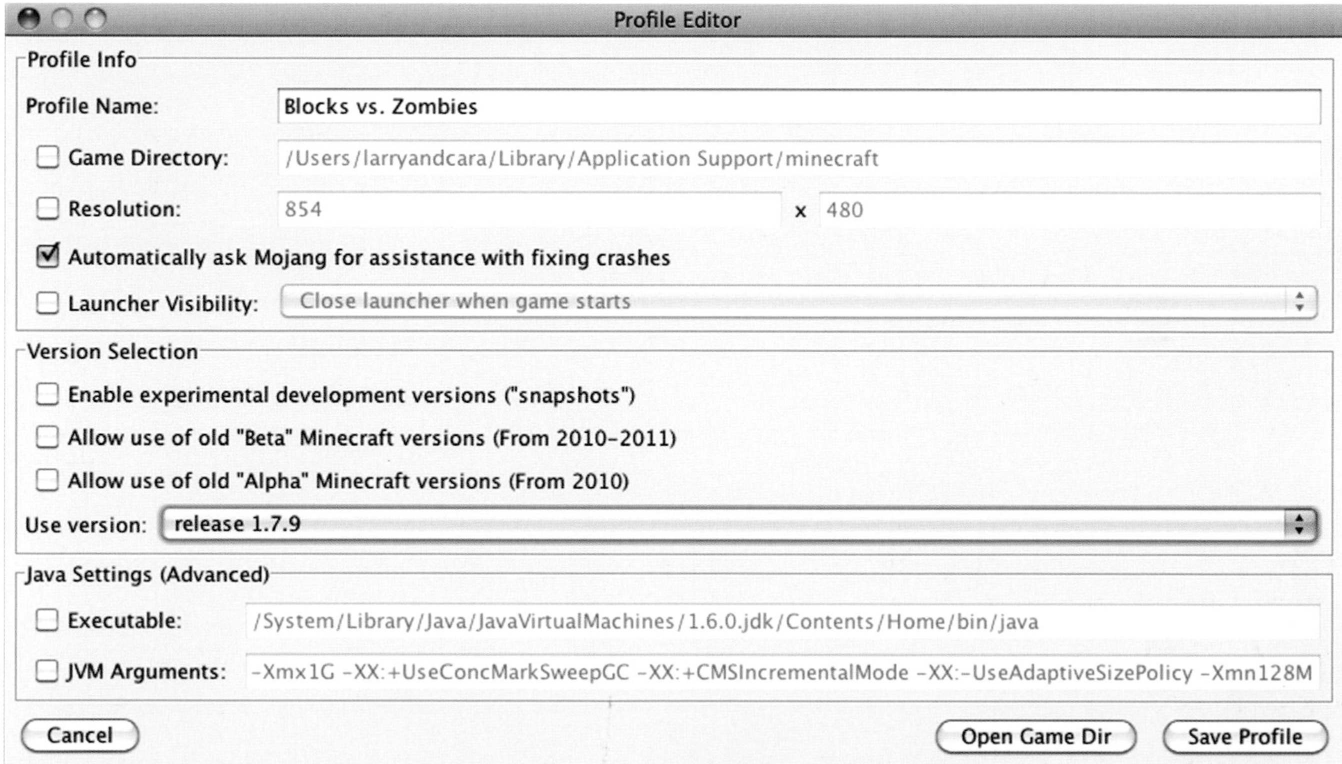

Some servers run on older versions of the game. Plants vs. Zombies is one example of a server that usually needs to be rolled back because it uses older command blocks to run the game.

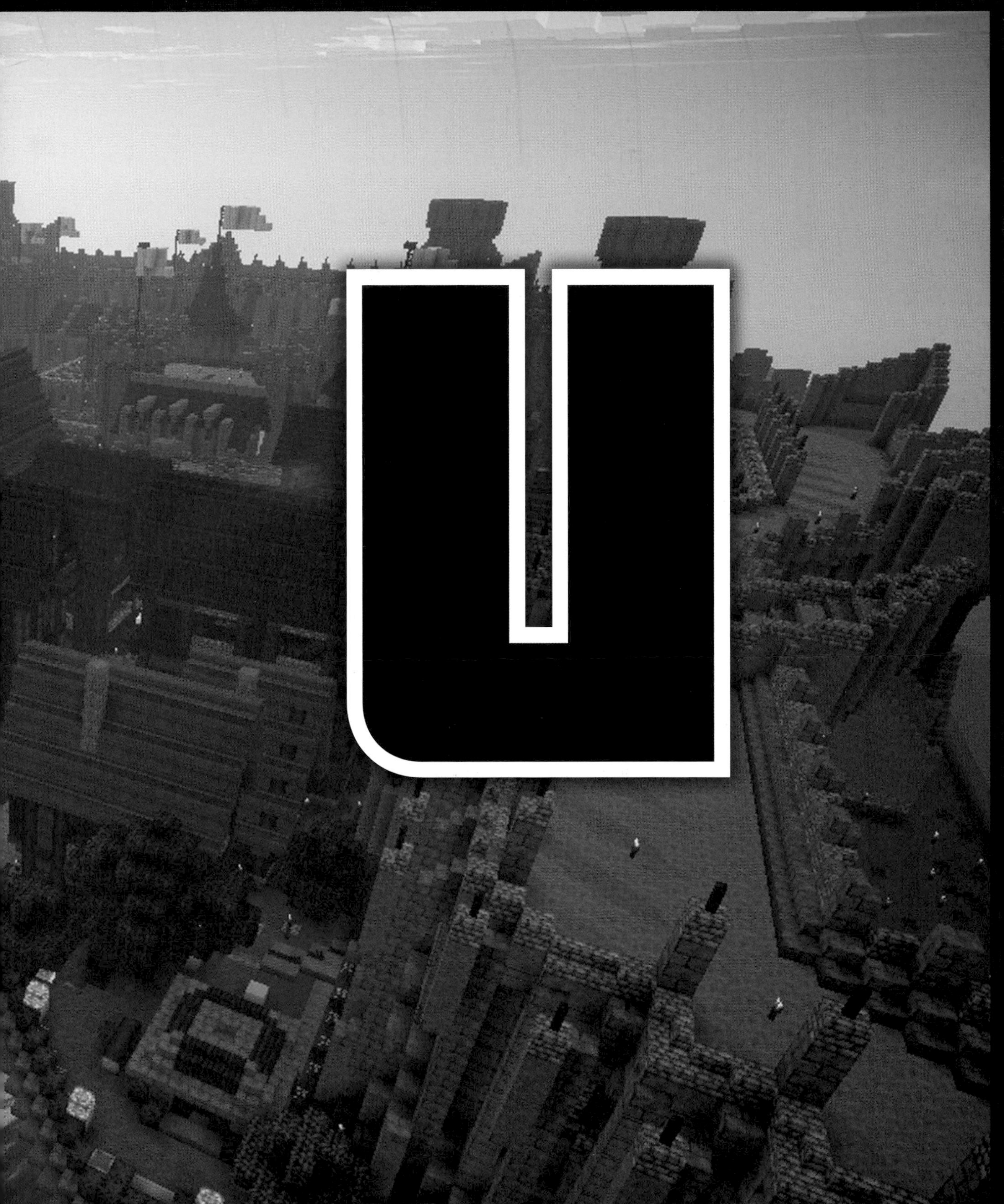

U

UNCOVERY:

Uncovery is a Survival server that is made for experienced players. Since 2010, Uncovery Minecraft has created a mix of Vanilla survival Minecraft and a multiplayer experience. Although the site offers a working economy, it also sticks to the rules and mechanics the single-player experience offers.

Uncovery Minecraft is known for its friendly and helpful player base as well as for its safe and stable environment that attracts many kids along with their parents. The site runs on donations and doesn't charge fees to play or upgrade features.

Heavens' Reach is a medieval city in Uncovery with a fort in the center.

A complete Roman city created in Uncovery.

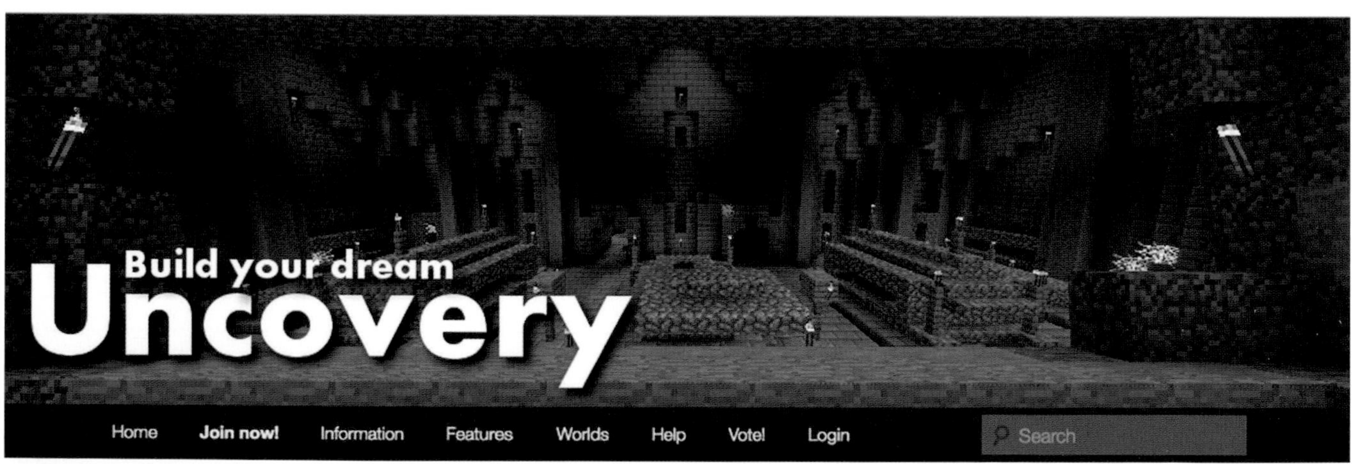

Uncovery attracts serious survival gamers. It also showcases some impressive and creative builds.

UPTIME:

Multiplayer gaming servers are known to crash from time to time. Look for server lists online that give you uptime stats so you know how dependable the server will be before using it. Good Minecraft servers have 95 percent uptime or more, while the best servers have over 98 percent uptime.

JacWiloh has charred to a well-done "JacWilo

V

PARTY GAMES 1

14
G 13
V 12
11
E eft: 694 10
R Left: 4 9
Time: 00:22 8
7
6
5
8/8 4
5★ 3
2
www.hypixel.net 1

steak!

VAMPIRE GAMES:

Multiplayer games incorporate kids' favorite villains, and that includes the blood-sucking vampires we love to hate. There are a wide variety of vampire mini-games out there, including the terrifying hide-and-seek game, VampireZ where humans hide from vampires and vampire players get to sink their fangs into opponents to convert them to vampires. If you're squeamish, you may not love the look of this game: severed heads and pools of blood are part of the scenery.

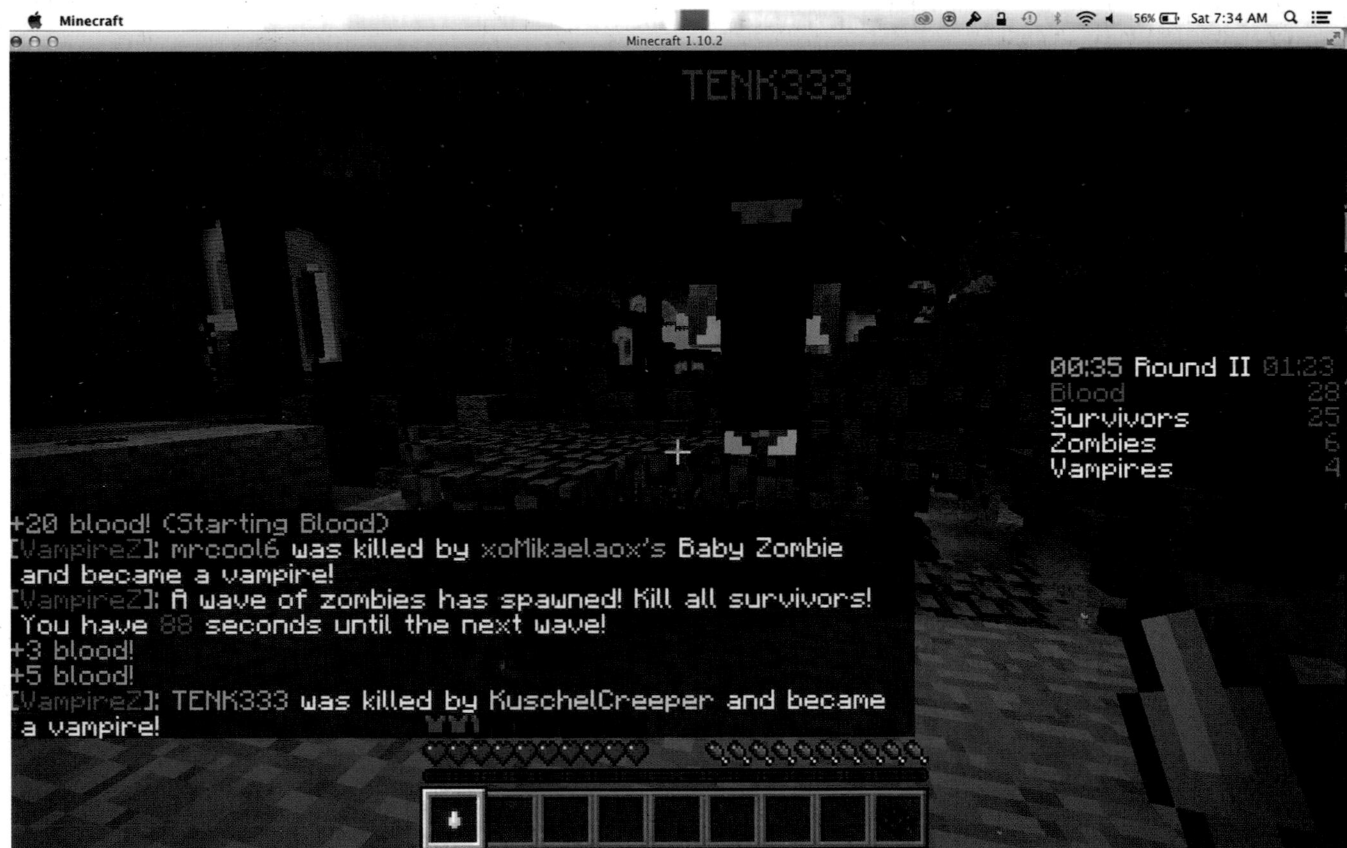

A VampireZ player is killed and instantly turns into a zombie.

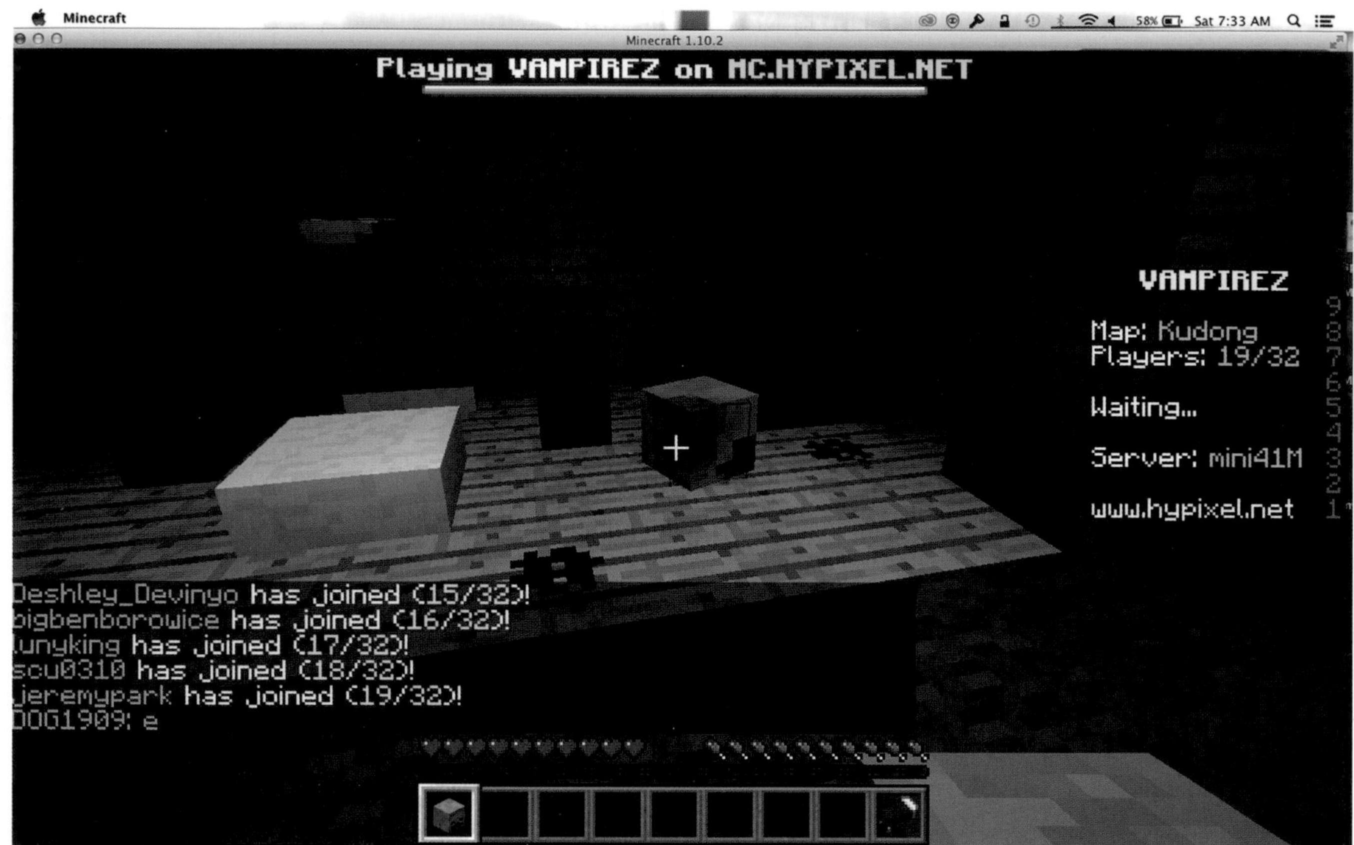

Prepare to see dismembered heads and pools of blood when you play the vampire attack game, VampireZ.

VANILLA:

The official server software published by Mojang is called Vanilla. It is always up-to-date, because it is always released at the same time as the Minecraft updates. There are even snapshot (development) versions of Vanilla available. Vanilla multiplayer servers offer the exact same experience as a single-player survival game that doesn't use **plugins** or **mods** but with the added benefit of multiple players.

VERSIONS:

Minecraft has evolved since it's earliest form (1.0 in 2011) and has already been updated and released in many different forms. Before you join a server, make sure that it can support your version of Minecraft. If the server runs on an older version of Minecraft, open up Minecraft and click "Edit Profile" to select a more suitable version.

VOLCANO:

Volcano is one of many quick-and-easy party games for players whose screen time is limited. Hop from block to block to avoid falling into the lava and you could be the winner of this action-packed multiplayer party game.

Multiplayer party games can be a satisfying alternative to longer, more complicated challenges. Volcano is an example of a quick-and-easy game to figure out: One false move and you could be swimming in lava.

Conne

Kicked whilst connecting to Lobby: You are n

www.

Back to

1.10.2
on Lost
white-listed ye
-list @
W.net !
erver list
W

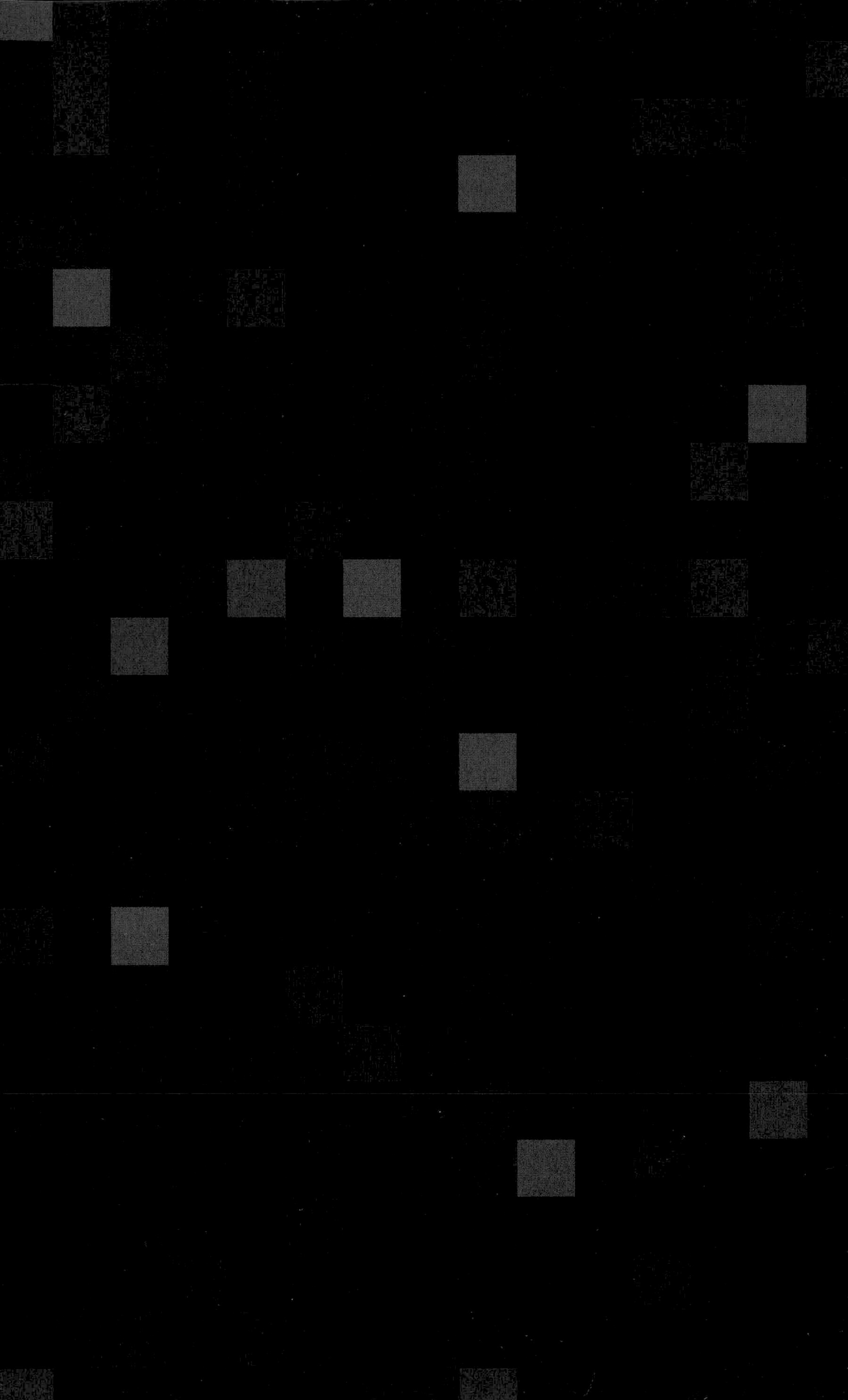

WHITELIST:

A whitelist is a list of players who are allowed to access a specific server. Servers use whitelists to ensure higher quality players on the servers and to stop **griefers**. Servers without a whitelist will probably have a lot of griefing going on. You need to be approved before you can join it. Often you go to the server's website and fill out an application and then wait a few hours or days. Applying for a whitelisted server can be a bit of a drag, but it does provide an extra degree of reassurance that all the players on the server are known to the server administrators. You can also create a server that has a whitelist so only your friends can join. If you try to access a whitelist server and you're not on the list, you'll get an error message if you try to connect.

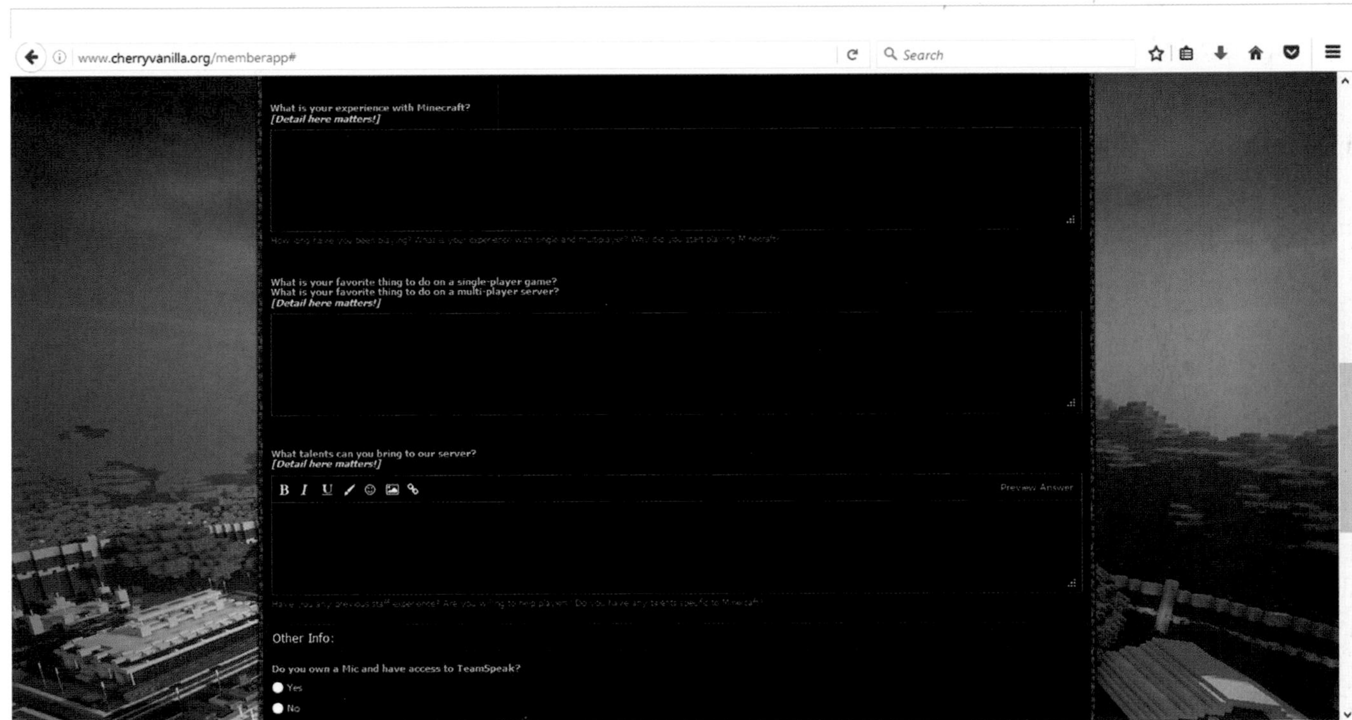

A whitelist application for a cherry Vanilla server. Once you're accepted, you can log on and play.

If you're not on a whitelist, you won't be able to access a whitelisted server.

WOOD:

Although wood can be a great tool for building, it should be avoided when building houses in Multiplayer mode. In Multiplayer mode, wood attracts griefers, who will easily burn down wooden buildings and steal whatever is inside.

WORLDGUARD:

Some servers, like Cubeville, offer the WorldGuard plugin to claim and protect your land. Say you've just created an awesome house, found a place to store your loot, or built a lovely flower garden, but you can't be there 24/7 to keep an eye on it. With WorldGuard, you can protect your area with a set of commands:

//wand—After you type this command, click on two opposite corners of your space and WorldGuard will define a square around it to protect.

//expand 5 u—This protects the area five blocks up from the ground in your defined area.

/region claim—After region claim, type in the region name, then your username before hitting enter. This makes the area yours.

/region select—Type in the region name after region select before hitting enter so you can make changes to the region you're protecting.

//expand 5 d—This protects the area five blocks below the surface you have claimed so that mobs, griefers, and anyone else who likes to dig can't get into your space from beneath it.

/region redefine—Type in the region name after typing region redefine and before hitting enter to save your changes and protect your land.

WRAPPER:

Wrappers like Multiplay Admin do not usually change the way you play a game, but they do allow server operators a better way to manage their server. Some provide uptime assurance or stats so server owners can make your gaming experience as smooth and enjoyable as possible.

X Y Z

X-RAY VISION:

There is a mod that gives you x-ray vision so that you can detect valuables more easily. Finding diamond, coal, and iron is a lot easier with the help of this mod. However, most multiplayer servers will discourage using this kind of advantage. X-ray vision is easy for admins to spot, and could get you banned from some servers, so it's probably best to resist.

YOUTUBE VLOGGER:

Most of the information you already know about MMO you may have learned from YouTube videos. Vloggers capture their gameplay online and comment as they play. You can learn a lot from these videos, but many many many of them have a lot of swear words and some may contain inappropriate content. It's best to follow a few good vloggers you know and trust. One good place to start is the Stampylonghead or Stampylongnose channel at www.youtube.com/stampylonghead. The vlogger known as Stampy Cat creates fun, family-friendly videos with challenges, storylines, and information that can make you a better player and entertain you at the same time.

ZERO.MINR:

Jump, climb, and run to your heart's content here without fear of crafting, killing, or defending yourself. Zero. Minr is an advanced

Exercise your Minecraft avatar with some sweet Parkour moves.

ZeroMinr offers new places to jump and travel.

Parkour map that takes a lot of practice and patience to master. Once you enter this realm, you'll find yourself falling to your doom. A lot. Really a lot. It's frustrating at first, but stick with it.

ZOMBIE APOCALYPSE:

A zombie apocalypse is just one of many plugins that can be used and enabled when you play on multiplayer servers. Servers like Towncraft have enabled the plugin to add the risk that a swarm of zombies will appear at 9 p.m. You need to defeat a certain amount of zombies before morning to earn an achievement—the admin of each server decides what that number will be. A zombie apocalypse gets you more drops, lets you earn in-game achievements, and adds to the fun if you're into the whole zombie battling thing.

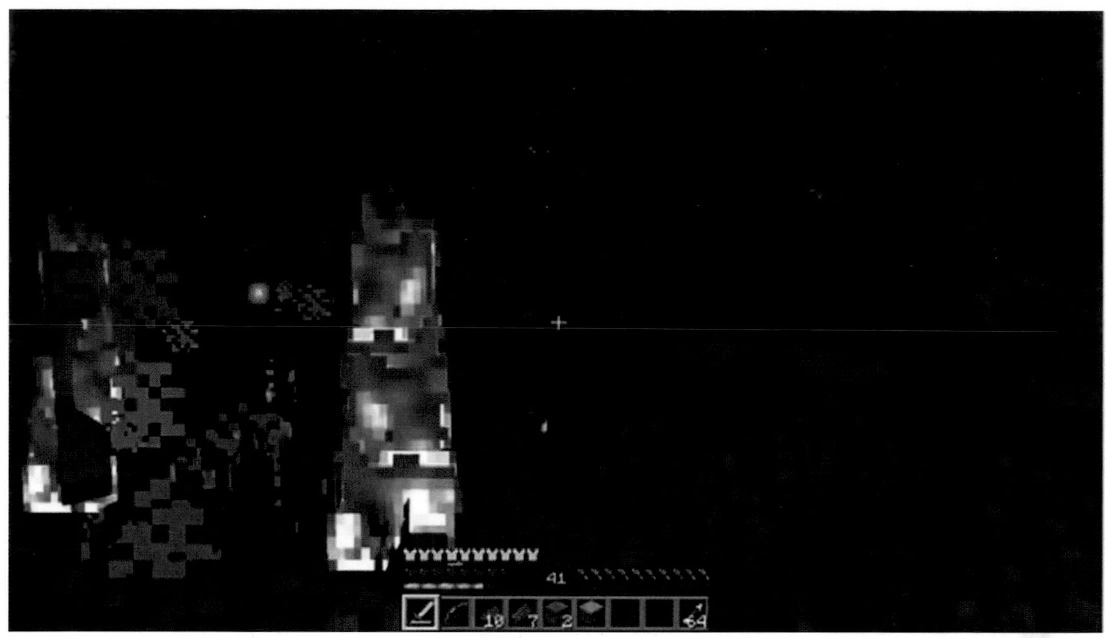

Survive and own the Apocalypse!

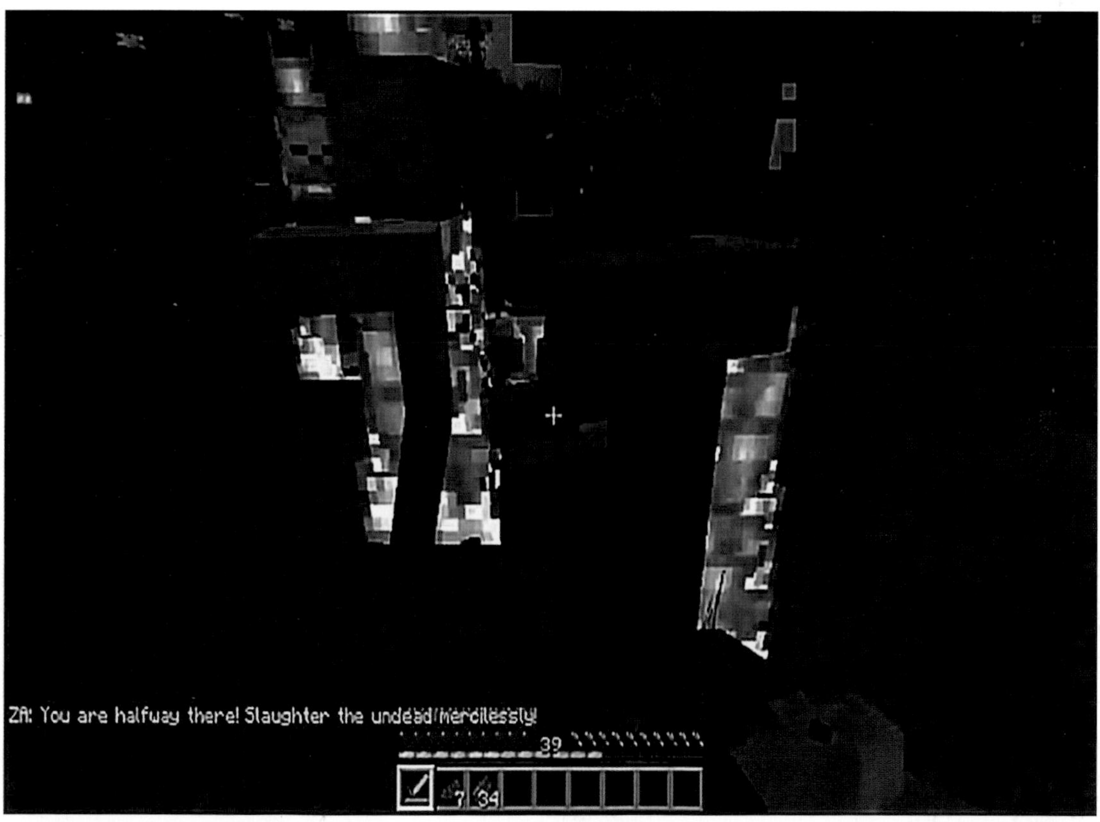

Drop whatever you're doing when the zombies start to swarm.

ADDITIONAL RESOURCES FOR KIDS AND PARENTS

www.howtogeek.com/school/htg-guide-to-minecraft/lesson15

Minecraft.gamepedia.com

commonsensemedia.org

http://www.planetminecraft.com